SHORTS
FOR THE
BEACH

J.M. Fisher

Shorts For The Beach

"J. M. Fisher needs to put away his dirty laundry."

— Jacque E. Shorts, *Wedgie Today*

"It's a great beach read. Be sure to wear your suit so as not to arouse the authorities."

— Butt McCraken, *Sandflea Review*

"I lost my Bermuda shorts in the triangle—they just disappeared. Now I'm nude."

— Richard M. Nixon, *San Clemente Beach Dispatch*

"This book covers more than the annual *Sports Illustrated* swimsuit edition."

— Howard Cosell

JMFISHER.COM

Author's Note

Editor: Sharon Massen, Ph.D.— trents1940@aol.com
Any errors or omissions are the sole responsibility of the author.

Final Arrangements (Revised, 2014) previously appeared in *Return To Luna*. Courtesy of Hadley Rille Books, 2008.

The following stories previously appeared in *If I Stand Under It Will I Understand It?* published December 2008. All were revised 2014.

Life On Mars? — The Value Of Deception — Dr. Chopstick — Their Ought To Be A Law — Why On Earth Did We Build It? — On Truth And Lies In A Global Sense — Joe's Place — Does Poetry Matter? — The Magic One.

ISBN – 13: 978-1496087331
ISBN – 10: 149608733X

Thank you to my writing critic group, and the Gulf Coast Writers Association, for your inspiration.

Also by J. M. Fisher

Desire

Awarded the Gold medal for Humor and the
Silver medal for Adult Fiction by the
Florida Authors and Publishers Association, 2013

Dangerous

Please visit jmfisher.com

CONTENTS

"A lot of young people have great difficulty committing themselves to a relationship or to a career because of the feeling that once they do, they're trapped for a long, long time."

— Mary Catherine Bateson

"So do us old guys . . . that's why we refuse to die."

— J. M. Fisher

For My Nana

The Man Who Loved Words

Paige Turner rolled her wheelchair across the dingy and frayed carpet and parked inside Samuel Johnson Swink's cubicle.

"Are you okay?" she asked.

"Yes," Sam replied. He stared at a spreadsheet displayed on his computer screen.

"Are you sure?"

"Yeah."

"Why do you let Kendrick treat you that way?"

"I don't know." Sam looked at the fabric wall of his work space. It was barren except for a solitary photograph of his mother.

Paige eased closer. "It wasn't a bad mistake . . . and we caught it before it went to corporate."

"I told him that." Sam adjusted his glasses and glanced at Paige. "You know how he is—I'm responsible." He turned his attention to the numbers on the screen.

"That doesn't give him the right to browbeat you—"

"It's my job to make sure the numbers are accurate. And they should be. Kendrick has every right to demand one plus one equals two."

"That doesn't give him the right to treat you like an idiot," she said. "Everyone heard him yell 'you'll never amount to anything.'"

Sam did not respond.

Then she said, "It was my screw-up and I want to tell him."

"No." He turned his chair so he could see her. "It may be a cliché, but I don't want to throw you under the bus."

"But why should you be lambasted?"

Sam looked at the ceiling. "You shouldn't worry about me." He had silently counted the holes in the ceiling tiles many times and he started again.

"But I feel awful that you're taking the blame. . . . Will you at least let me take you to lunch?"

Paige waited.

Sam counted.

Then she said, "You'll have to ride the elevator with me."

Sam stopped his count and thought to answer no. He turned his head toward her and hesitated. Then he said, "Yes."

At noon, Samuel Johnson Swink, self-conscious about his receding hairline, bypassed the stairwell and boarded the office elevator along with Paige Turner. When the elevator doors opened at the ground floor, Paige touched the gold crucifix hanging from a chain around her neck.

Sam and Paige sat at the only empty table, next to the kitchen door. A young waitress, bubbly like champagne, took their lunch orders and they were alone.

Paige studied the lines on his face. "Thanks for sticking up for me. I'm sorry Kendrick took it out on you."

"It's alright. He's said worse and I've survived."

"It might be me, but I think he always has sharp words for you, even when nothing is a problem. Do you think so?"

"He's getting old—maybe he has less patience because his time is running out."

"There is so much stress at the office," she said. "I'd like to quit.

Have you ever thought about it?"

"I can't—I've been at Saltmine Industries for 25 years—just a few more and I'll retire."

"Well, if he talked to me like that, I'd sure tell him where to stuff it." She calmed and chose her next words with care. "I admire your patience, Sam. I'd never be able to hold my tongue like you."

"I've always found it best to stay quiet . . . no need to make it worse with words I would regret."

Sandwiches and chips arrived.

"Even though I don't like him," Sam continued, "I must accept reality." He took a bite of his pastrami on rye. "Because I've got no where else to go."

Paige wondered why, but did not want to inquire. She took a bite of her tuna on rye, chewed softly, and dabbed a napkin around her mouth. Then she asked, "What are your retirement dreams?"

Sam sighed and looked at the light fixture hanging above the table. It was cheap decor in keeping with the modest ambitions of the café owner. He glanced at her and said, "I haven't given it much thought—everyone says I should travel, but I don't like going alone."

"I don't like traveling alone, either."

The waitress stopped at the table to check—everything was okay.

After the waitress moved away Paige asked, "Any places you'd like to see or people you'd like to visit?"

"I don't know," he said. "Maybe some day I'll wake up with an urge to go somewhere—but I don't have any thoughts as to where I'd go."

"Really?" She wanted to know more about Sam's family but did not want make him uncomfortable. Instead she asked, "Do you have any hobbies?"

"I used to collect stamps."

She smiled. "So did I! . . . U.S. or Foreign?"

"It didn't matter."

"I loved foreign ones," she said. "My great aunt sent me postcards as she took a round-the-world trip. My favorites were from Indonesia because it was so exotic. . . . I still have my collection. Do you?"

"No, I donated it to charity several years ago."

"Why?"

"I don't know . . . just lost interest . . . like childhood dreams."

"Maybe your dreams can re-awaken?" She arched her eyebrows.

"No." He sipped his iced tea and thought his short response might be misunderstood to be rude. Then he asked, "How about you—what do you like to do?"

"I like to read—and I like to write poems."

"What do you write about?"

"Oh, I'll try my hand at anything—but mostly nature," she said. "I try to write two poems every week. . . . Did you ever write poems?"

"I once wrote a poem for my mother."

"What was it about?"

"I don't remember much of it any more."

"I'm sure it was beautiful and full of love." Then she added, "Would you like to come to my poetry group? We meet Saturday nights. Everyone is welcome."

"No. . . . Thank you. I wouldn't be any good—I haven't written anything since that day."

"Why did you stop?"

Sam put his sandwich on the plate and looked at his lap. "I don't want to talk about it."

"That's okay, I didn't mean to get too personal. . . . Let's talk about something else," she said. Then, "What did you want to be when you were growing up?"

"A fireman."

"Really?"

"Yes. . . . How about you?"

"A ballet dancer." She smiled. "I was, until . . . ."

"What do you mean?"

"I was paralyzed."

He did not know what to say to her.

"I don't mind telling you, Sam—it happened so long ago." She paused and added, "My partner dropped me during rehearsal and I traded ballet slippers for a wheelchair."

He still did not know how to respond.

"For years I was bitter and angry," she said. "Finally, I accepted God's will and moved on with living. . . . Do you believe in God?"

It had been a long time since Sam had thought about God. Her question made him feel uncomfortable, as if he were archaic and obsolete.

The check arrived and Sam took it.

Paige frowned. "I invited you to lunch."

"Thanks, but I must."

As they made their way along the crowded sidewalk Paige said, "You didn't answer my question about God."

"I'm not sure. Some days yes, some days no." Then it was his turn to change the subject. "What do you like to read?"

"I read all kinds of books," she said. "Fiction, romance, poems."

A scraggly-bearded slacker, walking while texting, ran into Paige's wheelchair.

"I'm sorry," she said as she maneuvered the chair backward with the control stick.

The slacker glanced at her and moved on without speaking. Paige and Sam continued onward and threaded their way through the lunchtime crowd.

When the sidewalk cleared and it was possible to talk, Paige said, "Sam, my books are great friends—they never have an angry rant or are rude—like some people we know." She smiled, looked up to him, and added, "And like foreign stamps, the words of a book sweep me away to places of adventure, hope, and love."

"Yes," he said, "but words can be mean and hurtful. . . . That's why I like numbers—you can't insult someone if you call them a 72 or a 242."

"Unless you are referring to a woman's age or weight."

He laughed and said, "You're right."

"And you're right about words that carry a harsh tone," she replied. "But you *must* look at the positives—so I focus on poetic words that are noble and majestic—like God."

They came to a crowd of business suits and hipsters who blocked the sidewalk while waiting for a seat inside a trendy bistro. Most of the crowd stared at cell phones, which made it difficult to maneuver the wheelchair, so Sam and Paige took separate pathways.

After the sidewalk was clear she asked, "Do you believe in God, Sam?"

He didn't answer because he thought about how he cried to God after his father died of a heart attack—shortly after he'd given his mother the only poem he ever wrote.

———

When Sam arrived at his cubicle the next morning, he found a pink envelope on his desk. He opened the envelope and found a poem, handwritten in neat script on a white card.

Happy words for the boy were lost
Leaving youth coated with frost
Numbers only, they made their mark
Numbers cold, like the dark

We can break the icy clutch of number
For a home minus love is only lumber
Let's find warmth on a regal sailing trip
With you, my man of words, as Captain of the ship

He re-read the unsigned poem several times and put it back inside the envelope. As he did, he noticed the letters S-W-A-K written in light pencil on the back of the envelope.

He put his head down and thought about what he could say to Paige. Then he shook his head no and tucked the poem inside the jacket pocket of his suit.

———

Two days later, Sam plodded up the stairs to his apartment which was located inside a brick building—the place he had lived since the passing of his father. He held a bag of groceries with one arm, turned a brass key in the lock, and was home. As he re-stocked his refrigerator and pantry, he thought about his mother, a file clerk, and recalled her words, "Everything has its place."

The pantry, like the numbers on a spreadsheet, was orderly. Each can of food sat in a row, single-file, oldest first, labels facing straight. He placed the groceries in their proper place and noted the additions on a list taped to the inside of the pantry door, continuing his mother's tradition.

He sat at the two-person kitchen table and pulled out his pocket watch. It was an antique timepiece, worn smooth, that once belonged to his father. As Sam looked at the watch face, he remembered his father and what his father often said about the watch: "It's always exactly right."

Then Sam retrieved Paige's pink envelope from the refrigerator door and returned to his chair. He turned the envelope over and read the neatly printed letters S-W-A-K. He thought about what to do and his eyes grew misty.

And then, Samuel Johnson Swink—an only child who was taught the virtues of toil and sacrifice by parents who were refugees from war-scarred Europe—had a happy idea.

The next morning Sam's heart raced as he walked familiar sidewalks and stairwells to the place where he organized and compiled numbers. The place where he triple-checked each column because Kendrick numbers had to be exact because Kendrick and numbers were never to be corrected.

He arrived at his cubicle at the appointed time, reliable as his father's watch. However, instead of staring at numbers postured on an unnamed spreadsheet, Sam watched for Paige. She arrived twenty minutes late and he went to her cubicle.

"Good morning, boss," she said. "I'm sorry I'm late. The bus broke down again."

Sam did not want to discuss her tardiness. He smoothed his tie and said, "I enjoyed our lunch. . . . And your poem. Thank you."

"I'm so glad you did. I worried I might have offended you."

"Oh no, Paige. Your words are beautiful. I posted it on my refrigerator door."

"Really?"

"Yes, it's the only poem anyone ever gave to me." He took a deep breath and added, "I don't know how to ask—I mean . . . would you like to go for a walk by the lake tomorrow?"

A smile, worthy of prom night appeared. And Sam heard, "Yes."

They came to a bench overlooking an easy grassy slope that led to the water's edge. They stopped and silently admired the view— together. And on a spring Saturday by the lake, Sam felt a swoon for a girl confined to a wheelchair.

When the mood was right for conversation Paige asked, "Do you really like working with numbers?"

"Yes."

"Why?"

"Because numbers predict," he said. "They can be controlled and ordered to behave—unlike life. So . . . yes."

She thought about his comment for a time and felt a desire to argue the point. Instead she said, "You should write poems. . . . When I write I forget about my condition."

Sam felt a wave of sadness as he imagined Paige as a promising ballerina. It was the same melancholy he felt when he thought about his father.

He didn't know what to say to Paige so he took her hand in his. She intertwined her fingers with his and gently squeezed.

After a comfortable moment she asked, "Why did you change the subject when I asked you about your poem, Sam?"

"Because my father died."

She gently squeezed his hand again.

Then he thought about the last time someone squeezed his hand like she did—that time when he asked his mother, *"Did Dada die because of my poem?"*

And he remembered his mother's hug and her tears and, *"No, Sammy. . . . Dada loves your poem and he reads it everyday. . . . You are his little angel and mine, too."*

Then, for the first time, Sam gently squeezed Paige's hand.

She took a deep breath and smiled. Then she said, "Sam, everything that has been felt and dreamed is found in poetry—and every poem is made of words found inside a dictionary—but your hand in mine is beyond all words."

He was unsure of what to say. He finally responded with, "Words have failed me many times . . . that's why I like numbers."

Paige wanted to help Sam understand and she chose to be strong with her reply.

"Sam, we need words . . . they define our human spirit and our existence."

He did not answer. He looked away and began to silently count the branches on a nearby tree.

Then she said, "Words give wonder to beauty—they give us a way to share our beautiful world."

He stopped counting.

She added, "And words give surprise—because—you never know what they will bring your way."

He thought for a moment and said, "Numbers are predicable and can be organized. They represent the unvarnished truth—and a sum total that brings closure."

A small bird swooped close to their right, startling both of them. They watched it land on a branch of the nearby tree. The bird chirped once and darted away.

"But numbers have no sense of adventure," she said, "and words tell a story long after we're gone. That's why the words engraved on a headstone carry so much meaning—they memorialize humanity—numbers can only represent the time."

Sam watched a sailboat move away from the shore and disappear into the afternoon haze. He wished he could take Paige into that boat and away from the windowless cubicle but he didn't know how to tell her.

After a long silence she said, "Sam, I'd like to dip my toes into the lake."

"I don't think we should get that close to the water. . . . What if you get stuck?"

"Stuck! Do you think I'm like an old stamp on an envelope?" She laughed and pushed the wheelchair control stick. The chair moved toward the lake and she called over her shoulder, "You're weightless when you swim."

"It's too dangerous. I'm not strong enough to free you from the mud."

"Yes, you are." She stopped. And then over her shoulder she said, "Do you believe in love, Sam?"

He didn't respond.

She turned and faced him. "It's the story that all little girls dream. I know I did once. . . . Please . . . we can do it."

He still did not know what to say.

She smiled and said, "If you won't take me to the lake . . . then let's go to Bali."

There was a long pause and he asked, "Bali?"

"Yes."

"Why go to Indonesia?"

"My aunt wrote that it's beautiful . . . and because you've got poems to write . . . unless you really believe my chair will get stuck."

Sam felt the beauty of words and the magic of surprise.

They had ice cream in the afternoon and soon it was time for Sam and Paige to go their separate ways. They held hands and waited at a corner light. The light turned green. Sam kissed Paige on the cheek and said goodbye.

He stepped into the crosswalk and called out, "Enjoy your poetry meeting tonight." Then he crossed the street, waved, and turned toward home.

A bus driver, distracted by a fistfight between two passengers, did not see the wheelchair parked on the sidewalk. The bus jumped the curb and Sam heard the screech of the tires. Sam turned, and in a heart attack second, his life was touched by death. Again.

Paige Turner had reached the end.

When Sam finally arrived home, he took the pink envelope off the refrigerator and sat at his small desk in the living room. He turned the envelope over and stared at Paige's special hand-written letters—S-W-A-K.

———

Four days later, Landlord Noah Webster heard a knock on the front door. He rose from his threadbare recliner, checked the peephole, and saw two policemen. He fumbled with the latch and opened the door.

"What can I do for you?" he asked.

The older policeman said, "I'm Officer William Barnes and this is Officer Gilbert Noble. Does Samuel Johnson Swink reside in Apartment 2B?"

"Yes. . . . Is something wrong?"

"We've been asked by his employer to do a welfare check," Barnes replied. "He doesn't answer the door. Have you seen him recently?"

"No . . . but that's not unusual. Sam is a quiet man and lives alone. Would you like me to let you into his place?"

"Yes."

Webster led the policemen to the apartment and knocked on the door. There was no answer, so he inserted a key, cracked open the door, and called out, "Sam? . . . Sam?"

There was no response.

"Sam, the police are here."

There was no response so Webster swung the door open and all three men entered the living room. There was no sound. No smell. Nor anything out-of-place—just library silence.

The officers checked the apartment. Everything appeared normal, as if someone put things away because of superstition. Sam's wallet, keys, and eyeglasses were on a shelf next to the front door.

"This guy sure is clean," Barnes said as he checked the tiny kitchen. "Not a scrap of paper or even a dirty coffee cup."

The pantry door was ajar. Barnes opened it and saw the food inventory list.

"Look at this," he said. "Catalogued and orderly—not the type of guy to wander away on the spur of the moment."

"He's a good man," Webster replied, "took good care of his mother. She had diabetes and her feet got so bad she couldn't walk. He never left her, except when he went to work or shop. Never missed the rent."

"Does he have any family or friends?" Barnes asked.

"Only his mother and she died three years ago. Sam doesn't socialize."

Officer Noble went into the living room and looked over the modest desk.

Barnes pulled a pen and a notepad from his shirt pocket and asked Webster, "Did he have any recent visitors?"

"Not that I'm aware of."

"Did he mention meeting someone or going anywhere?"

"No. Sam kept to himself. I'd only talk to him now-and-again when I'd come up to repair something."

"Do you know of any reason we should suspect foul play?"

"None at all."

Barnes looked at Noble, who stood near the desk, and asked, "Anything?"

"Not much—just a pink envelope, a poem, and a scribbled note."

"What does the note say?"

Noble picked it up and read it aloud, *"Dear Paige, Thank you for showing me the love found in words. All of my love, Sam."*

Noble took a closer look at the note and added, "It also has the letters S–W–I–N–K below his signature."

"Better leave it where it is," Barnes said. "I'm sure Borders will want to see it."

Barnes turned his attention back to Webster.

"We'll turn this over to Detective Borders," he said. "He'll be in touch with you soon. Please leave everything in the apartment as it is." He pulled a police business card from his pocket and handed it to Webster. "Call us if he returns or if you learn anything we should know."

Samuel Johnson Swink never returned to his work cubicle or his apartment. And his body was never found.

The missing person investigation conducted by Detective Borders uncovered no clues as to his whereabouts. No airline ticket purchase. No activity on credit cards or bank accounts. No unusual email or cell phone activity and no forwarding address.

There was absolutely no trace of Samuel Johnson Swink and nobody would ever know what happened to him. . . . Except for the unexplained appearance—in every dictionary worldwide—of a new definition for an old word:

swink *n. archaic Old English, 12th century*
1. Labor, drudgery.

2. **S–W–I–N–K** *acronym — Sealed with Indonesian newlywed kisses*, as in the phrase, *"Let's set sail for Bali. S–W–I–N–K."*

Inspired by *Defining the Word*, the story of Samuel Johnson's first dictionary of the English language, by Henry Hitchings.

Somewhere Inside Hurricane Dennis

13:00 Hours

FORT MYERS, FL—The hysteria has arrived. So lots of folks, including me, are milling about the wine aisle at the supermarket. All of us are urgently asking: *What do you serve with wind—red or white?*

Nobody seems to know for sure, but the bag boy's suggestion got my vote after he recommended the weekly special—three bottles for 7 bucks. I bought two red, one white, and a bag of cat food.

On the drive back to my island home, I observed harried workers covering exposed windows with plywood, and a well-dressed reporter, along with a cameraman, interviewing sunbathers at the beach.

I also listened to reports, from a car radio blaring in the adjacent lane, that my house may be in extreme danger, and my person may be in mortal danger. Adding to the festering angst, weather forecasters reported Hurricane Dennis has the *potential* to strengthen from a Category 1 storm into a Category 5.

I'm taking it all with a grain of salt and three bottles of the cheap stuff—because the news wants to keep me glued to the station so I can't miss the advertisements for hurricane-related products and services.

I'm okay with the sincere expressions of concern for the safety of my fellow citizens and the repetitive public service advisories to take precautions before the storm arrives.

However, I wish the authorities would honor the tradition of naming hurricanes after females—storms were more exciting when they reminded me of women I coveted—especially if the one to ravage my male domain was named Lolita.

The water company began installing a sewer system in my neighborhood yesterday. Because the approaching storm has shut down all activities, except storm prep and waiting for storm updates, I figure the timing is an ironic twist of fate made possible by the God of Random Construction Delays—because this project was designed to carry water away from my house and prevent flooding.

The construction workers have dug two long trenches in front of my home; one on either side of the driveway. They also left a back hoe parked on the tree lawn. So, if Hurricane Dennis gets ugly, I'll fire up the heavy equipment and bury the storm debris in the trenches.

The latest forecast advises the storm surge might go as high as seven feet above the high tide mark. My house is two feet higher than that, so I will not need to swim out the front door, or cut holes in my roof, to escape. However, if I want to retrieve the newspaper, or start the back hoe, I'll need waders.

14:00 Hours

I tried to check the National Weather Service hurricane update on the Internet, but the server crashed because it was too busy. At my place, the winds are 15 mph from the southeast, blue skies have turned gray, and heavy rain fell for three minutes. The cats are fine and my groceries have been unloaded.

17:40 Hours

My television is broken—the result of channel surfing while practicing real surfing in my living room. That means my sole connection to the outside world is a dial-up Internet connection and a cell phone—along with the simulcast of the television news on an emergency radio.

Because I'm an island recluse, I have an advantage over the newsroom staff at the broadcast studio—I can look out the window and see what is happening without the analysis offered by Jim Nimbus, News Team One weather personality.

However, I enjoy listening to Nimbus as he updates anxious viewers about the storm. He is in his element as he rattles off humidity percentages, rainfall amounts, wind speeds, storm track speeds, and barometric pressures.

Adding to the deluge of Nimbus numbers, his co-presenters tell listeners their man Nimbus has a vast knowledge of weather and a special meteorological certificate. I think all he possesses is an uncanny ability to remember numbers—repeating them over-and-over, like a pocket calculator run amok.

19:45 Hours

Carol Itolduso, a serious anchorwoman, is also featured on the News Team One simulcast. Listeners are frequently advised she is bringing us, "the absolutely latest, updated storm news, just as soon as a new storm update is available, if not before."

There seems to be more than storm stress in the newsroom because Itolduso repeatedly interrupts Nimbus which causes him to lose his train of thought—so he has to repeat his list of numbers. Again.

Nimbus just informed me the latest storm track movie will play continuously on the lower right hand corner of the television screen—although I cannot see it while listening to the emergency radio.

Itolduso has become increasingly concerned as the afternoon wears on. After the last update, and replay of the storm movie, she cried out, "Oh the humanity!"

Nimbus was not fazed by Itolduso's outburst; he remained cool, calm, and collected. It makes me wonder if his meteorological certificate may offer him Superhero protection from the impending doom.

My hurricane wine has twist-off caps. The wine is great because I saved some real dough by purchasing the blowout special. However, I am mildly concerned about offering cheap wine if a friend stops for a visit, or a stranger seeks shelter from the storm—oh, the humanity.

The sky is filled with foreboding gray clouds. A light rain is falling and lightning and thunder are performing with gusto.

The cats and I are fine. Mozart is in the CD player and I'm thinking about taking a soak in the tub. I've put off attaching the hurricane shutters until tomorrow—and will only install them if the reporter on the beach has been blown away.

My latest dilemma: Refuse service was cancelled and my trash was not picked up—but it's dark, raining, and I've drunk one bottle of wine, so I won't retrieve the cans rolling around the street.

21:30 Hours

A strong, gusty wind is blowing the rain sideways. I can't see much of anything out the windows, so I must rely on the simulcast to tell me how bad it is outside.

Or, I can turn on the porch light and open the front door.

Nimbus claims the storm is intensifying and it may become a

Category 6, a number which is not on the intensity scale.

Lois Toldmeso has joined Carol Itolduso at the anchor desk. Amazingly, Toldmeso has Itolduso's strange desire to frequently interrupt Nimbus with repetitive comments, including this gem: "It looks like it will be *very* bad this time, Jim."

To which Nimbus replies: "Yes, and it looks like we'll get hit *very* hard this time."

23:55 Hours

My storm anxiety has forced me to tune out Nimbus and tune the emergency radio to a different channel—the local Christian radio station. Unfortunately, I have discovered God's channel is simulcasting Nimbus's competition. This television news broadcast is covering a "bigger, more powerful hurricane," than the Nimbus storm.

Mace Twain, the new television weather dude, has just announced the storm is *"very* gigantic." In fact, Twain reports it's so big that he upgraded the storm name to George—skipping over all names that begin with the letter E or F.

Lucky for me, the emergency radio batteries died, so I was relieved of duty—listening to storm updates.

But I'm not out of the loop. My cell is active with tweets, texts, and the occasional call from friends far away. There have been storm updates, jokes about wet reporters holding metal umbrellas, and a few oddball tweets concerning the welfare of Jim Nimbus.

The house is strong and holding up to the storm. Other than flashes of lightning, loud thunder, and howling wind gusts, everything I can see is okay. The second bottle of wine has been enjoyed and the cats have disappeared, probably sleeping under the bed or soaking in the tub.

During one of my patrols, I saw my potted orchids, which hang from the arbor near the front door, swinging wildly in the wind. So, I stripped to my naked self and entered the fray in a rescue attempt. As I stepped out the front door, rainwater gushing from the roof hit my bare behind. It was mighty cold and *that* has repercussions.

Against all odds, and cold water, I fought my urge to cover up and moved the orchids to the ground. I just wish I'd switched off the porch light.

03:10 Hours

I was awakened by the cats who were playing with wooden chess pieces on the tile floor—at first I feared the house was breaking up in the raging storm.

A check of my cell indicated the worst was over—except for a series of tweets concerning the fate of Jim Nimbus. From what I'm able to piece together, Nimbus lost his mind after 24 hours of non-stop storm coverage.

Apparently, just after I went to sleep and before the storm made landfall, Nimbus had a nervous breakdown. He lost it after the broadcast took a live telephone call from Erwin Masky, a viewer reporting on storm damage in the Everglades.

During the call Masky said, "Mr. Nimbus, did you get your meteorological certificate from a home study course? . . . I got the matchbook cover right here—it says: *Make Big Money—Be a TV Weatherman.*"

Nimbus's reaction to the caller's question involved the flailing of arms, disco-like body gyrations, and denials in a high, squeaky voice.

Itolduso tried to get Nimbus to calm down by saying, "Jim, according to Mace Twain, it's a *very* big storm and we're going to get hit *very* hard."

In response, Nimbus hurled his pointer stick at the blue screen and walked off the set. Then, from somewhere off-stage, Nimbus yelled for a cameraman and a vehicle so he could "report live from the eye of the storm and escape the blather of my female news co-anchors and swamp people."

The crazed weatherman was last seen, wearing a plastic trash bag for rain protection, broadcasting live. This is a clip of that broadcast:

The Last Stand of Nimbus

"This is Jim Nimbus, Action Weatherman, reporting live from somewhere on Sanibel Island. It's dark, windy, and raining hard. The roads have become impassible for my station-issued vehicle, but I'm certain Bob and I are reporting live from the eye of the storm."

"Jim, this is Lois Toldmeso at the studio. It looks like you're really getting hit *very* hard out there."

"Yes, Lois—"

The camera picture suddenly jerks, swings, and tries to focus on something in the background.

"Jim!" Itolduso yells. "There is something *very* wicked coming your way!"

Nimbus turns and says his final words: "My God, it's bad out here—a naked man flew past—clothes ripped away by the wind—reporting live from eye of the stor—"

The on-location broadcast signal is lost and viewers see Itolduso at the anchor desk. She is visibly shaken by the raw violence and sits dumbfounded.

Toldmeso handles the situation with professionalism. She calmly says, "Looks like Jim got hit *very* hard."

A moment later, Itolduso regains her composure and asks, "Did you notice any shrinkage, Lois?"

Aftermath

In the morning, when the sunshine streamed through the window, I woke up groggy and hung over. I crawled out of bed and made my way to the bathroom and looked in the mirror.

I witnessed a horror—three days of beard growth and uncombed hair. No doubt the eye of the storm passed directly over me. But at least I was alive—although the house had no electricity and no running water.

I combed my hair with my fingers, grabbed the last bottle of wine, and set out to survey the damage. I looked out the front window and saw downed trees, broken branches, and orphaned palm fronds covering the yard. To my surprise, I also saw roofing shingles sticking out from tree trunks and a turkey buzzard pecking at a small dead animal.

Worst sight of all? My trash—scattered all over.

I surveyed the damage a second time and then looked across the street at the old warrior's place. His yard was covered with debris but his house and flagpole stood tall. The Stars and Stripes and the Marine Corps flag were still flying—tattered and torn—proving that Marine was at his post.

I went to my front door and tried to open it. I pushed hard to move away the piled-up junk and wormed my way into the hot, humid air and sunshine.

Nothing was unscathed and nothing was recognizable. Garbage, palm fronds, tree branches, and pieces of other houses were scattered everywhere. A red kayak, from parts unknown, stuck from my hedge like a dagger that had been plunged into a chest. Plastic patio chairs, broken and dirty, littered the yard, tossed like cigarette butts from speeding cars. A helicopter, flying a search and rescue grid, was the only thing in the sky.

I worked my way down the driveway, crawling over downed trees and stepping around storm debris. As I approached, the turkey buzzard lumbered aloft, leaving his carrion for my inspection. I was unable to identify the dead animal, so I turned it over with my shoe and discovered it was a toupee.

I moved to the street and spotted a Smart car, covered with mud and parked haphazardly on the tree lawn. Nearby, on the ground, was an abandoned video camera that had a *News Team One* sticker.

There was rustle and moan so I cautiously approached the trench that had been dug by the city workers. Inside the trench was a man sprawled on his back. His clothes were muddy and soaked, but I was able to read the insignia sewn on his shirt: *News Team One Bob.*

I stepped into the trench and bent down to check his pulse. His eyes were wide open, as if he'd witnessed an unspeakable horror, and his breathing was shallow.

I touched his shoulder and said, "It's alright, buddy. The storm has passed."

"We were hit real bad," he muttered. "The Earth opened up . . . I was swallowed alive."

"Are you in any pain?"

"No. . . . Where's Jim? . . . Where's Jim?"

I stood and surveyed the area. On the opposite side of my driveway I saw a mud-covered penny loafer, jutting upward from the other trench. The shoe was attached to a foot and the foot had a black cable wrapped around the ankle.

I approached and saw, in the bottom of the trench, two legs sticking out from a pile of debris. I frantically pulled at the debris and uncovered a hand which held a microphone. I removed more debris and saw a face obscured by remnants of a plastic trash bag. I started to pull the bag away from the head but stopped, not wanting to see a dead body. The bag moved and I realized the storm victim was alive.

I pulled the bag away and revealed a man who was oddly familiar yet strangely different. His head was over-sized and completely bald—but I still recognized Jim Nimbus, television weather personality.

The noise of the chopper grew louder and the sunshine was hot. Nimbus motioned for a drink, so I held my bottle of wine to his lips and he drank greedily. Then I pulled it away, fearful there would be none left for me.

Nimbus fumbled for something in his front pocket and motioned for help. I fished out a pack of cigarettes and matches. I lit one for him and stuck it between his lips. He nodded in appreciation and I pulled another and lit it for myself. That's when I noticed the matchbook cover read: *Join the Jim Nimbus Fan Club—Be a Nimbecile!*

I took a long draw, put the matches in my pocket, and studied the man. He appeared to be okay, except for the large beads of sweat that had formed in the cracks and crevices of his bald head.

"What happened?" I asked.

He blinked many times and tried to speak.

I bent close to listen.

"A naked body flew past," he whispered. "The ground swallowed Bob—like a snake—then the ground swallowed me."

He caught his breath.

The chopper was landing nearby, making it difficult for me to hear.

"Like a snake," he whispered. "Swallowing . . . slithering . . . the horror . . . the horror."

The chopper settled to the ground—the bright *News Team One* logo painted on the side. Several people disembarked and moved toward me. Two women, with enormous heads, seemed oddly familiar yet strangely different. They were Lois Toldmeso and Carol Itolduso, followed by a cameraman.

Toldmeso reached me first. She had the wild-eyed look of a reporter interviewing a crazed man who held a bloody hatchet.

"This is Lois Toldmeso reporting live from the eye of the storm," she said. "News Team One has found a survivor of last night's devastating storm. Our Jim Nimbus and cameraman are still missing . . . but I see their vehicle nearby."

She turned to me and said, "Sir, destruction is everywhere—yet you survived. What happened out here?"

I looked over Toldmeso's shoulder and saw the American flag and the Marine colors in the distance. My posture stiffened.

"Tell us the truth about what took place," she insisted as she thrust the microphone into my face.

I looked at her. Then at the flags, tattered and torn, but still flying.

"The truth? You want the truth?" I said. "No. . . . You just want to hype and distort the truth so you can make money." I turned and walked away.

Semper Fidelis, Marine.

Cast of Characters

Hurricane Dennis	The Ex
Cameraman Bob	Ex's New Beau
Jim Nimbus	Ex's Attorney
Carol Itolduso	Ex's Former Attorney
Lois Toldmeso	Ex's Spiritual Advisor
Narrator	Himself
Retired Marine Warrior	Narrator's Attorney

Final Arrangements

A National Space Society "Return To Luna" Fiction Contest Winner (2008)

MOON STATION *CONCEPTION* 14 March 2034—06:12—Coordinated Universal Time (UTC).

I pulled my hand away from the carotid artery of Commander Garret Henderson's neck, where my fingers had searched for a pulse. He was warm, but lifeless.

I listened for a breath.

Nothing. No sound of life. Just like the vacuum of silence outside on the Moon.

"Houston . . . Henderson is gone," I said.

My wireless comm picked up the words and two seconds later my voice echoed in Mission Director Alex Oberg's headset at Mission Control.

My earpiece cracked with Oberg's response, "Say again, Colonel?"

"He's dead." My voice sounded distant and disconnected from the reality.

"Dead? . . . Did we copy?"

Henderson was face-up in his bunk. I gently shook him again, hoping he'd sit up, bellow his baritone laugh, and announce, "Gotcha, Bird!"

But his empty green eyes told me that he'd embarked on a new voyage.

"Say again, Colonel," Oberg said.

I looked down and away. "There is no pulse. No respiration."

"We're going live."

A red light glowed on a camera mounted in the upper right corner of the stateroom. The motorized device swivelled and pointed at Henderson. His face was covered with a stubble of gray and white whiskers, the lips were blue, and the mouth was relaxed.

"Are there signs of trauma? Hemorrhaging?"

"No."

I closed his eyes with my fingertips.

Then I stared at Henderson and felt the aloneness—I was the only man alive on the Moon.

It was 4:13 a.m. in Houston when the words, "Henderson is gone," arrived at Mission Control. Immediately, the stoic professionals activated contingency plans to determine the cause of death, insure my safety, and reassure the public there was no risk to Earth.

However, I was not worried about the storm sweeping Mission Control. I felt sad and strangely calm as I looked around Henderson's home away from home. It was a place I rarely ventured without an invitation, just as he avoided mine.

A live image of Earth, captured by a camera outside the station, appeared on the wall-mounted flat screen. A picture of his wife, Elizabeth, stood on a small desk. The ornate silver frame was positioned so he could see her before going to sleep and upon waking.

Henderson's hair clippers were also on the desk. A blinking green LED indicated the battery was re-charged by the station's solar array.

The clippers reminded me of our arrival on the Moon, five months ago. Just two regular guys, Commander Garret Henderson, U. S. Marine, and me, Colonel Nelson Avery, Air Force Flyboy—the first to occupy a permanent settlement away from Earth.

Henderson memorialized our place in history by permanently setting his hair clippers to the Number 1 buzz cut—because—as he said upon our arrival, "When you are first, there is no other position."

He shaved his head every other morning. And afterwards, as if it were a ritual practiced only by Marines, he'd remark how great it was to rid himself of the overgrowth.

 Then he'd chuckle and say: "Let me lawnmower your head, Byrd. High and tight never goes out of style on the Moon."

My answer was always the same: "No thanks, Commander. My bald cranium is too ugly—I'd scare away any girls who might come to visit me."

Now, as I watched the silent blink of the LED on the hair clippers, I whispered, "Commander, I'd like that trim today. . . . Care to fire up that cheesy weed whacker and have a go?"

But the green blink, like a lighted candle placed in a room after someone has passed away, did not reply.

"Colonel," Oberg's voice broke the silence, "We need you to lock the hatch and close the ventilation while we assess the situation."

"Okay, Alex."

"I'll report to you in fifteen minutes as to what's next."

I stepped into the narrow corridor and pressed a switch to close the door to Henderson's quarters. After the door slid into position, I went to the Command Center and activated the computer controls to close the vents and seal the room.

The Command Center was the only place inside the station with a window. The window was a 4x5 plexiglass affair that afforded us a view of the dark crater floor and the stark, sunlit mountains 19 kilometers in the distance.

Henderson and I had spent most of our waking moments in the Command Center because we could study the magnificent view which was never the same. Even though the outside cameras presented live pictures to the flat screens inside, we preferred the direct eyeball connection to Earth.

As I took in the view, I recalled what Henderson told the engineers who designed *Conception*—the same Erector Set personnel who insisted the station be covered with a 3-foot layer of Moon regolith—moon dust and lunar soil—for protection from dangerous solar radiation.

"You Erectors buried us alive so we can live," Henderson fondly reminded them. "But please expedite that 360-degree view copula . . . so I can get my head out of the sand."

A buzzer sounded and Oberg's voice came over the loud speaker: "Colonel Avery, we need you to move the body to the medical ward."

"Roger," I replied.

It was time for me to attend to the business of Earth—time to place Henderson on a sterile exam table and remove his clothes. Time for a machine, controlled by a tech in Houston, to collect blood and tissue samples. Time for Henderson to be a lab rat.

And time for me to accept my original Moon mission ended with Henderson's final breath. A mission for which I had trained almost twenty years.

I left the Command Center, went through the galley, and returned to Henderson's quarters. The door slid to the left with a soft swish and I entered his stateroom.

"Right this way, Commander," I said as I hefted his six-foot-two frame over my left shoulder; his body easy to manage as it weighed only 40 Moon pounds. As I carried him to the Medical Ward, I remembered our jokes about "feats of strength versus that mediocre strong dude, Incredible Hulk, back on Earth."

I placed him face-up on the exam table and undressed the body. I removed his watch, wedding ring, and a gold cross that hung from a chain around his neck.

A robotic arm, commanded by an operator in Houston, disengaged from a mount on the ceiling and scanned the entire body and moved to the left arm. A rotating mechanism turned and a needle appeared and drew blood.

The robotic arm moved to the abdomen and a new, six-inch needle appeared. It was inserted into the stomach and a sample was taken. After additional samples were drawn from the lungs and heart, the arm moved away from the exam table.

"We're ready for you to turn the body," Oberg said.

I approached and whispered, "Okay Major Tom, time to roll over for the man." I took a hold of his left arm and gently turned him over. His right arm swung away and dangled. I shifted the body and put the right arm on the table.

Once again, the robotic arm scanned the body, bathing it in an eerie blue light. The arm moved away and returned to its mount in the ceiling.

"The exam is complete," Oberg said. "It's time to put him in refrigerated storage."

I pushed a button on the console and a small door on the wall opened upward. A flat drawer extended, next to the exam table. I retrieved a body bag from a locker, laid it out on the flat drawer, and moved the body into the bag.

After I positioned Henderson's body, I took one last look at his face before zipping the bag closed. Then I pressed the button again.

The drawer retracted, the door closed, and Henderson was gone.

I went to the galley, made a pot of coffee, and poured a cup. No sugar. No cream. The coffee was strong and unyielding—like the Commander and the Moon landscape.

I sat at the galley table where we shared meals and thought about the Moon, Henderson, our accomplishments at the station.

Conception was humankind's first step to colonize another world. Or, as the talking-head detractors preached, "a disrupter of the pristine."

The station was located on the rim of Shackleton Crater, near the Moon's South Pole. The site had been selected because it was bathed in perpetual sunshine, providing a power source, and the crater floor was in perpetual darkness, providing a water-ice resource.

The water-ice deposits, brought by asteroids and comets over the eons, were *Conception's* life-support currency and enabled expansion of the station. Eventually, *Conception* would house 50 settlers, who would pioneer the extraction of raw materials and live where humans first settled the final frontier.

Our charge was to greet the autonomous space transports that brought additional modules and consumables, and oversee construction of the station.

Every 20 days, a transport arrived and made an automated landing. Then robotic tractors, operated by us, or the construction boys in Houston, unloaded the cargo.

The tracs, as they were called, did all of the heavy lifting necessary to attach a new module. After a visual inspection by Henderson and I, power latches secured the module to the existing structure. Tracs then scraped regolith into piles and covered the addition.

Henderson and I were the go-to guys, the human element able to troubleshoot and override when the red lights flashed on the machines.

Henderson, a big man, hailed from a linage of space pioneers. His father retired from NASA after 35 years. In his last capacity, he served as the Propulsion Director for the James Webb Space Telescope—a spacecraft that peered into deep space to study places where the building blocks of life might be discovered.

Henderson's grandfather was another rocket cowboy. He flew on the Space Shuttle in the late 1980's and tested the Manned-Maneuvering Unit, and as a result, was one of the few men to experience free-flight in space.

Henderson said of his grandfather's adventure, "He plunged into the void and returned to say: 'I flew alone, untethered from humanity—untethered from life—but never—untethered from God."

Now home and humanity were a lifetime away and fate had intervened—Henderson would forever be known as the first human to die away from Earth.

And I was left to wonder if our time on the Moon would be marked by something more than to be known as the dead man space construction team.

I took my coffee to the Command Center to wait for Oberg's next update. He soon advised I was authorized a rest period, so I tuned a flat screen to television programming from Earth.

No formal announcement had yet been made and the all-news channels made no mention of my predicament. I played space-channel roulette, and I stopped on a broadcast of an old Q and A between a class of third graders and Henderson and me.

The camera cut to a close-up of a little blonde girl who asked, "Why do we go to the Moon, Mr. Commander?"

Henderson always enjoyed questions from children—perhaps because he and Elizabeth never had one of their own—and this time was no exception.

He smiled and said to the classroom of youth and innocence, "Exploring and learning are in our DNA. . . . When we stop exploring, we stop learning. . . . That is why God gave us an imagination."

I ended the television feed and looked out the Command Center window.

After a long meditation, I buzzed Houston and said, "Alex."

"Yes, Colonel?"

"I need quiet time—I'm turning off the comm." I flipped a switch on the unit attached to my waist and disconnected from Earth. I went to my stateroom, set the comm on the desk, and laid on my bunk.

My thoughts jumped back to the last time Henderson and I explored outside the station. It was a "liberty trip," taken just two days ago. We went to our favorite lookout, a place Henderson named Waikiki Beach, to share the view of Earth.

On that day, the Commander switched off his comm as we sat on a rock outcropping. The black sky held only a single item of interest: a basketball-sized Earth, low on the horizon, just above the bleak moonscape—a dreamy spectacle.

From our vantage point, the Earth appeared as a smooth blue-and-white ball, with none of humanities' achievements or imperfections visible.

After a long silence Henderson said, "It's just a swirl of human emotion. . . . That's the fundamental problem, Bird. . . . Emotions."

We sat without speaking, looking at home. Maybe Henderson knew his time would soon arrive because he raised his right arm, pointed at Earth, and broke the silence:

"Bird, either you grow and change, or sit dead as a rock on the river bank while the water flows past. That's why we are here—we *must* migrate throughout the Universe and we *must* leave our mark."

A buzzer signaled and it brought me back to reality. Mission Control wanted to talk. I went to the Command Center, activated the comm, and saw Oberg on the display. I pressed a switch and a light indicated the camera beamed my picture to Houston.

"Yes, Alex."

He adjusted his eyeglasses and said, "Colonel, we have considered your immediate evacuation via *Rescue One* . . . but we will keep you quarantined at *Conception* until we understand what caused Commander Henderson's death. It may last several weeks."

"I expected that."

"Nelson, you are ordered to remain inside the station—it's too risky to venture outside alone. . . . And you must keep the comm open at all times."

"24/7?"

"Yes."

"Fabulous."

Oberg looked away and continued, "We'll bring Garret home on *Rescue 2,* which will launch in about 12 hours. Autopsy results will allow us to decide how long your quarantine will last.

"In the meantime, autonomous transport *Clarke* is in en-route and will touch-down as scheduled. All station construction has been suspended until further review."

"Have you informed Elizabeth?" I asked.

Oberg pressed the mute button, turned to his right, and spoke to James Duffy, second-in-command at the CAPCOM station. He reactivated the comm.

"She has not yet been notified."

"Garret asked me to speak with Elizabeth if we had an

emergency."

"Roger that, Colonel. . . . We are waiting for the preliminary medical report before notifying next-of-kin and the press. We'll arrange for you to speak with her after she has been contacted."

"What about tomorrow's public Q and A?"

"Cancelled. The Agency is scheduled to make a formal announcement later today." Oberg shifted in his chair. "Tomorrow, we'd like you to make a video statement for the folks back home."

Seven hours later, Mission Control buzzed me that Elizabeth was ready for a conference. I activated my stateroom console and seconds later she appeared, seated alone at a table in her home near Houston. Behind her, a large digital picture frame displayed a picture of Garret and Elizabeth as newlyweds, standing on a white sandy beach.

Elizabeth smiled tentatively and she held a tissue with her left hand.

"Hello," I said.

"Hi Nelson," she replied in her Tennessee accent.

"I'm sorry, Elizabeth. Garret loved you very much."

She sniffled and closed her eyes. "I didn't know how hard this would be . . . even though long ago I accepted Garret might die doing what he loved. . . . I knew that." She glanced away and then at the camera. "Before every mission, I'd tease him and tell him my Major Tom better always come home. . . . Now he won't . . ."

"Major Tom was a good man and good friend . . . loyal until the end."

She wiped her eyes with the tissue.

"Elizabeth, Garret had a message for you in case something happened," I said. "He told me he was going to surprise you with a trip to Hawaii for your twenty-first wedding anniversary—to celebrate the best years of his life."

Elizabeth bent her head down and held back tears. An off-camera voice said something I could not understand and she turned to listen. Then she turned to the camera.

"Nelson, Garret wore a necklace with a gold cross—his Mother gave it to him before he left for boot camp."

"Yes. . . . I have it and will deliver it to you, just as soon as they let me off this rock."

"No," she said. "He wanted to leave it on the Moon."

"I understand, Elizabeth."

"Nelson, I must go. Thank you." She pressed a button and her image vanished.

Ten minutes later the comm lite flashed and Alex appeared on my screen.

"Colonel Avery," he said, "regarding Commander Henderson's personal effects—we must remind you the International Moon Treaty of 2024 prohibits astronauts from leaving personal mementos of religious significance on the Moon. You are ordered to return all of Commander Henderson's personal property to Earth."

Oberg waited but I did not reply.

Then he added, "The Agency cannot politicize this mission with a controversy about religious symbolism."

"I know the drill, Alex."

I slept poorly that night, thinking about Henderson and the mission. Early in the morning, I rose and went to the Command Center—to disable the motion-activated cameras in the Ready Room, the airlock, and the vehicle bay.

Then I went straight to the Ready Room and sat on a metal bench in front of pressure suit 2B—the white one with a blue stripe on the arms and legs.

After I reassured myself about my plan, I stepped into the suit, fastened the gloves with a twist, and pressed the button to close the hard back plate. I pulled the helmet over my head, placed it in the ringed metal collar, and turned it a quarter-turn to seat the latch.

The suit automatically pressurized and activated the life-support system. The hum of the air circulation fan started and the heads-up displayed suit vitals and GPS coordinates.

I stepped into the airlock and used the manual hatch mechanism to override control from Houston. I pressed the switch to de-pressurize and watched the LED's move from green to red as the air pressure fell. It would take thirty seconds for the airlock, which led to the vehicle bay, to be emptied of air.

My headset cracked with the voice of Alex:

"Colonel Avery, we report the airlock has been activated. Are you preparing to—"

I flipped off my comm.

I entered the vehicle bay and opened the main hatch to the expanse of a desolate, gritty, and ancient Moon. The harsh sunlight lit the far wall of Shackleton Crater; its razor sharp edge contrasting with the blackness of space.

I walked to the left side of a parked trac, slipped into the driver's seat, buckled the lap belt, and flipped the manual start switch. The electronics came alive with an auburn glow and the power cable automatically decoupled.

I pressed the accelerator and slowly drove down the aluminum ramp and onto the Moon. I steered the trac to a worn pathway—a path that was marked by a hand-lettered sign Henderson had posted, with an arrow pointing to Waikiki Beach.

After a ten-minute drive, I arrived at the overlook, parked, and turned off the power. The glow of the instrument panel disappeared and I sat and took in the view for a long while.

I unbuckled the lap belt and pivoted to the left. Then I placed my left boot, and then my right, on the surface of the Moon.

As I stood, I remembered something Henderson told me once:

"Bird, every time I step onto the surface, I hear those immortal words, 'One small step . . . '"

I felt the soft crunch of dry regolith under my boots and watched as gray grains of moon dust floated upward and then rained down— the grit created by the impacts of micro meteorites and solar radiation over the past 3.1 billion years.

I traversed a few meters to a rock outcrop that Henderson had named after a bar in Hawaii: *The House Without a Key*.

I leaned against a large boulder and sat on the dusty lunar regolith. The area was crisscrossed with our boot prints—some distinct and clean, and others disturbed by steps taken on later visits. I saw some of Henderson's large boot prints—they marked the places where he stood as the first human since the creation of the Moon.

I looked into the jet black sky. The half-lit Earth was just a few degrees above the jagged outline of Shackleton Crater on the far horizon and it resembled the Moon rising over the Diamond Head landmark near Waikiki Beach.

With one easy sweep of my eyes, I saw all of the Indian Ocean, the Indian subcontinent, and Sri Lanka. I moved my gaze westward, to the Middle East, where conflict still raged. My eyes moved down and across the brown deserts and savannahs of East Africa, where humanity first learned to walk upright. To the left was the terminator, that eerie, in-between twilight which announced dawn across the cloud-covered, western portion of the African continent.

It only took a few seconds for my eyes to travel across the breadth of life that was Earth and across the history of humankind. And, in an odd way, I had just traveled faster than the speed of light.

My eyes returned to the wild grasslands of East Africa and I thought about how early man may have looked at the Moon, just as I now looked at Earth.

Perhaps that early man, like me, felt the same raw emotion when loss paid a visit—that deep sadness we feel when someone is no longer.

I fumbled with the velcro closure on the pocket of my left arm and removed Henderson's gold cross and held it with my right glove. The pendant and chain swayed in the bright sunlight.

I looked at the majestic Earth, which hovered silently in the dark sky, and thought,

There it is, Major Tom . . . the place of blue lagoons and coconut trees. . . . You'll be home soon . . . back to Hawaii and your Elizabeth.

I sat in the cold vastness of the stark, sharp vista—barren of green, red, or blue. Barren of any life, except Henderson, the Earth, and me.

Then I carefully placed the necklace on the rock with the gold cross facing Earth. It glinted boldly in the harsh sunlight.

I sat looking at home, and then, after a long while, I heard Henderson's voice echo inside my head, "Carry on, Marine."

Citizen Jack

The *Fort Myers News Dispatch* editorial staff quickly returned to business-as-usual after overzealous reporter Jack Tyler left the newsroom for the final time.

Tyler was last seen pressing long-winded goodbyes onto anyone who would listen. He chatted up customers waiting to place classified ads, a homeless guy loitering near the main entrance, and the newspaper vending racks on the sidewalk in front of headquarters.

"I'll miss this place," Tyler said, even to the inanimate objects of his affection. "And I'll miss that hottie, Lois Laney, even more."

Inside the newsroom, keyboards clicked as editors and reporters worked to meet tight deadlines, finally free from Tyler's daily distractions. Distractions that included Tyler's efforts to cajole staff to partake in gambling challenges; irrate phone calls from readers who complained about Tyler's articles; and lame attempts by Tyler to uncover a story bigger than Watergate.

Several female members of the staff expressed relief, mixed with sadness, that Tyler would never return to the editorial offices.

"He was a friendly man but he liked Lois Laney too much for her liking," said Ellie Sherwood, gossip columnist. "I saw him now-and-again at social events but he was never accompanied by a date. Sometimes it touched on the pathetic, especially after Lois rescued him one day at the office. I kinda felt sad for him—but only for a little while."

Despite working with Tyler in close quarters, Laney was surprised to learn Tyler referred to her as a hottie and that he would miss her.

"He was a sweet man but not always helpful," Laney said. "We had a few issues, but no blow-ups that prevented us from doing our jobs—I'm pretty sure I yelled at him only every *other* day."

When pressed to confirm rumors about an affair between Tyler and Laney, spread by the homeless man outside the main entrance, Laney grew defensive.

"Jack and I never had a relationship," she said. "And we certainly never had sex. Only one time did we ever discuss anything but our work—and that was when Jack asked what type of man I liked. . . . He got my standard answer: A big strong guy who can fly."

Tyler responded to Laney's brush-off with disbelief and bravado, typical of the male species.

"I thought Lois and I might someday date because she once told me she liked my cologne," he said. "And another time she said she loved my Christmas tie. . . . But I could never get her to forget about that other guy and I couldn't find any Kryptonite."

Laney refused further comment regarding Tyler's choice of cologne and ties except to say, "Don't ever whistle that Old Spice tune around me."

Tyler's days at the *News Dispatch* were filled with excitement and anger—his own and that of Editor Norton Walker, a 20-year veteran of the newsroom.

"I've never worked with a reporter quite like Jack Tyler," Walker said. "He constantly told me he was just days away from breaking news that would change history. He even said he'd be more famous than Watergate reporters Woodward and Bernstein—if only he could find a story."

Walker's discussions with Tyler often turned into shouting matches, according to some office staffers.

"One day he barged into my office," Walker said, "convinced the newspaper itself was part of a conspiracy because the newsroom knew about news before it was news and that he was going to blow the whole thing wide open.

"When I advised him it was our job to find news before it was news so we would have news to print each day, he yelled something about his time would soon come and then he walked out the door," Walker said. "It was not unusual behavior for him."

Tyler's conspiracy theory raised eyebrows outside the newspaper offices but they didn't gain traction with the general public.

"He told me it was eerie," the homeless man said, "how newspaper staff knew what would be news before it happened. He claimed Walker must make secret calls to Psychic Melinda, who haunts the newspaper morgue."

"Yes," Walker confirmed. "One day Tyler said I get my news tips from Psychic Melinda, the morgue ghost. Rather than fire him on the spot, I demoted him to writing obituaries—so he could spend more time with his Ouija board in the newspaper archives."

As with many down-then-up success stories, the demotion led to one of Tyler's most controversial articles and his eventual rise to the top of the political heap.

Walker tasked Tyler to write an obituary about a Fort Myers pioneer, Earnest Brett, who had recently passed. The story ignited a family feud which featured irate wives, wielding machetes, storming Tyler's cubicle at the newspaper.

"I don't know how they got past security guard Hightower," Tyler told the homeless man. "But all at once, I found myself outnumbered by three heavy-setters, wearing robes, house slippers, and bent on revenge. They looked as if they'd been awake all night and hadn't been inside a beauty parlor for six months.

"Each of them claimed to be the lawful wife of Brett," Tyler added. "Funny thing though—none of them knew each other prior to the obit I wrote—and for some strange reason they blamed me for uncovering the dead man's serial bigamy."

Lucky for Tyler, Lois Laney was at work in her cubicle, just a few feet away from the impending mayhem.

"I calmed them down," Laney said, "by telling them Superman was expected to visit the newsroom and they'd better freshen up in the Ladies room in case he wanted to take them for a flight around the city."

After Laney intervened, Tyler was able to slip out a rear entrance and hide out until Brett was buried. After the heat was off, Tyler returned to his cubicle and was summoned by Editor Walker.

"Why in the hell did you feature wives in your obituary?" Walker asked. "And furthermore, why even disclose he was a bigamist—don't you know it's in poor taste to speak ill of the dead?"

"Because it was true."

"And how did you know?"

"It just so happens I played pool with Brett a week before he died," Tyler said. "We made a bet the winner had his pick of the other man's wives. I figured, since I'm not married, how could I lose?"

"So what."

"Well, how was I supposed to know Brett's wives didn't know about each other?" Tyler said. "Did they really believe his lies about being a commercial fisherman who needed to spend long days and nights, alone and far out at sea, when he was actually hustling single women and pool players inside local bars?

"As a crack reporter, it was my duty to inform the good citizens of this community, and his wives, of this information after he passed away."

"Jack really was innocent of wrong doing," Laney said. "Too bad those women were angry at the news—I was surprised they blamed him for the betrayal of trust, but it's typical of the public to seek the death penalty for the messenger."

After his close call, Tyler's emotions for Laney grew stronger. According to Ellie Sherwood:

"He confided in me that he sent Lois a bouquet of pink rose buds for Valentine's Day. Lois never did figure out who put them on her desk, and I didn't have the heart to tell him that Lois thought they were from Superman.

"Jack said he gave them to her because she saved him from the machetes, but his gesture was more than a simple thank you. After all, he signed the card, 'Love, Anonymous.'"

Tyler's first story to leap to the front page came after he called Editor Walker one morning to report an invasion of rampaging reptiles.

"He phoned from home," Walker said, "and told me huge lizards were overrunning his house and his pearl-handled Colt .45 was of no use against the alien invaders from Mars.

"Then he said he was the only newspaper man on the scene and he wanted an exclusive because the story had real legs and he would become famous."

Walker agreed to put Tyler's story above the fold after he learned the Channel 7 news truck was parked in front of Tyler's home, preparing for a live broadcast.

"I had Walker convinced," Tyler later said, "that Channel 7 would scoop the newspaper on the story of wild iguanas overrunning the neighborhood."

Walker responded to the breaking story with the coolness of a battle-hardened newspaper executive.

"We are streaming your telephone call live over the newspaper Website," Walker told Tyler. "We've already pre-scooped the story—all before Channel 7 gets their antenna raised."

"But the invaders—"

"Jack, calm down, put on your fedora, and get an interview with those reptilian beasts—we'll have it on the Internet before the Channel 7 newsgirl finishes her pre-broadcast primp."

Unfortunately, the story did not give Tyler the War of the Worlds infamy he desired. However, it was a slow news day so the photographs he took of several six inch iguanas made the front page, and he was promoted to regular news coverage again.

After returning from the doom of writing obits, Tyler credited his crusty and skeptical mentor, Editor Walker, with excellent counsel.

"Walker taught me," Tyler said, "to go to town everyday and find out what is upsetting the citizenry. . . . It worked, but I had to become a bar fly to unwind after the day was done.

"And boy are there reasons for people in this town to be upset," Tyler added. "Just the other night an aged rock-and-roll star told me, 'There are rats on the west side and bedbugs uptown.'"

Other reporters questioned the validity of Tyler's quote by the rocker.

"I don't believe he met a member of the Rolling Stones at Bar Joey as he claimed," said Ellie Sherwood. "I think the truth is he got his head pushed inside a jukebox by some good old boys after he asked them why they were mad."

Tyler was often too enthusiastic interviewing angry people, hoping they would lead him to the story of a lifetime. His actions led some citizens to complain Tyler rubbed them the wrong way—as best expressed by those stuck in downtown traffic on a hot Friday afternoon.

"He jumped into the middle of the street with a video camera and demanded to know why I was mad at the traffic backup," said driver Mary Dake, 86. "Who does that young feller think he is, Geraldo? I should've flattened him with my Oldsmobile."

Other commuters that day agreed with Dake's assessment.

"I slammed on the brakes to avoid running him over," said truck driver Big John Dallas. "There was a traffic tie-up because he played Cecil B. DeMille shooting *Cleopatra*. Someone ought to tell him Main Street ain't that river in Egypt—but I imagine he would go into denial."

Despite the public outcry that his reporting style was sometimes worse than the news he reported, Tyler never let go of his dreams of fame and fortune. Perseverance finally paid off after Tyler teamed with Lois Laney on an investigation that changed history.

Laney had received an anonymous tip that a privately-owned sewage treatment plant might be responsible for polluting a local beach. The beach had been closed by city inspectors after testing showed elevated levels of a dangerous bacteria in the water.

The controversy grew to front-page status after the mayor demanded health officials "leave no toilet unchecked" in the search to find the source of the water pollution.

After Tyler reported the mayor's outcry, health inspectors expanded their pollution checks by making surprise examinations of toilets throughout the county—even if the bathrooms were occupied at the time.

The surprise inspections created lots of upset citizens who demanded Tyler be banned from reporting live about discoveries and activities.

"I couldn't believe someone knocked on the stall door and

demanded entry," said private citizen T. P. Whipple. "My uncle is in the toilet paper industry but I never expected it would infringe on the quality of my life.

"I was just sitting there doing my own business," Whipple said. "Suddenly a guy with a clipboard is peering under the stall door and says he wants to check the water quality.

"Then another dude, holding a microphone, looks down at me from the top of the stall and asks if I'm upset about the water quality toilet checks."

During their investigation, Laney and Tyler learned that other sewage treatment plants in the area might also have serious problems.

Editor Walker agreed with Tyler that it had potential to develop into a big story, so he assigned Tyler, and cub reporter Timmy Olsen, to examine all of the Environmental Protection enforcement files related to wastewater treatment.

After they were assigned the investigation, Tyler convinced Olsen they were only a few days away from stardom and a Pulitzer.

To prepare for his upcoming 15 minutes, Tyler changed his attitude and wardrobe. He threw away his Christmas ties, grew a three-day beard, and put on a pastel linen blazer, as he and Olsen went deep undercover.

Other reporters suggested that Tyler's wardrobe change was not just about the investigative report.

Again, Ellie Sherwood commented:

"I think he changed his stripes because he was trying to impress Lois."

Olsen and Tyler went incognito as they examined years of public records related to sewage odors, spills, leaks, and deferred maintenance at numerous wastewater treatment plants in the county.

"This doesn't pass the smell test," Tyler often told Olsen as they compiled a lengthy bullet-point list of environmental violations.

"It was an exhausting task," Tyler later said. "In the beginning, I thought Timmy and I might be like Crockett and Tubbs on *Miami Vice.*"

But instead of flying helicopters and driving go-fast boats, the two reporters worked at a small table buried somewhere in the bowels of the health department complex, "reading about fecal counts and odor complaints."

The work was so tedious that Olsen remarked, "Jack lost his mind on the third morning of the effort. He quit working and kept telling me to pull his finger."

Amazingly, the two reporters learned noncompliant sewage treatment plants are permitted to operate because there is no alternative.

"It's not like you can turn off the flow coming into the joint," Tyler said.

The investigation also turned up evidence that sewage plant environmental violations might be a statewide problem.

As a result, Tyler convinced Olsen to commit career hari-kari based on the vague promise the public had a "voracious appetite for stories about recalcitrant owners of sewer treatment plants."

But Tyler took things too far with Editor Walker. The two men nearly came to blows after Tyler demanded the investigation be expanded to include all the sewer plants in the state.

"It was a ridiculous idea," Walker said. "Made worse by his insistence the public wanted to read every gory detail for the next six months. It was the direct cause of his dismissal from the paper.

"He wanted fame too much," Walker added. "I told him to stop but he kept right on going. So I told him I was going to demote him to hawking newspapers at a busy intersection. My threat didn't work, and finally, after I removed his hands from my neck, I threw him out of my office."

Tyler was convinced his fortune lay in the sewers, so he left the newspaper with the assistance and support of Walker. Soon after, Tyler formed the Sewage Treatment Party and ran for governor on a pledge to clean up politics *and* the sewer system—because it's the same job.

"It's all those people who eat that bring this problem on," Tyler said at the press conference where he announced his hat was in the ring. "They diligently eat three times a day to bring forth things that change our world. . . . That's why I left the newspaper and have entered the political arena. I'm going to affect positive change and clean up the waste in politics—because, as my campaign slogan says—I've got the runs for governor!"

His campaign encountered a rough spell, which Tyler said was a smear campaign led by his former employer.

Tyler claimed Editor Walker encouraged Mildred Sneed, a victim of bigamy, to go public with her story about an affair she had with Tyler while he was a reporter.

"Somehow," Tyler said, "just after polls showed me winning by a nose, Walker placed this woman on the front page. Lucky for me, the public wanted politics and the sewers cleaned—so they paid little attention to Walker's bogus headline, which I categorically denied by telling the public I never wanted sex after I saw that woman."

The front page headline, "Sewer Man's Sewage!" ran above a lengthy news story, penned by Norton Walker. It featured a tarty interview with Mildred Sneed, the first of the three wives of dead Fort Myers pioneer and fisherman, Earnest Brett.

In the newspaper article, Sneed claimed she was the prize Tyler won after he beat Brett in a friendly game of pool.

"He won a night with me," Sneed said. "It made me real happy—I was looking forward to sex with a stranger because I hadn't had any for quite some time because my husband worked so hard out-at-sea.

"This Mr. Tyler came up the stairs and pressed the bell. I opened the door and saw a man reeking of a cheap fragrance and wearing a red Christmas tie with little green mistletoe designs. Not only that, he wore a light-blue, white pin-striped, leisure suit.

"I tell you, I was embarrassed for him because it was August and nobody in the neighborhood had their outdoor Christmas lights on! I was totally unattracted and I think the voters of this state need to know this about that Tyler man who wants to be our governor."

However, that interview and the accompanying newspaper editorial about Tyler's competence, also penned by Norton Walker, actually helped Tyler pull off the upset victory.

Walker wrote on the newspaper editorial page: *If you want to vote for the stinky, lousy-dressed Tyler, as governor, go ahead. But please remember his most noteworthy accomplishment during his tenure at this newspaper was an in-depth look at the sewage industry.*

He has absolutely no other accomplishments—business, political, or otherwise. As you cast your vote, this newspaper asks you to remember that reporter-turned-politician is no Clark Kent.

But voters connected with the common man, who proudly wore Yuletide ties during the summer, because he insisted a state house with clogged pipes required the biggest plumbing snake available and a man unafraid to use it. He won the governorship twice—each time by a landslide.

After he retired from politics, Tyler wrote a book titled, *Why I Celebrate Christmas Year 'Round*, which stayed on the best-seller list for two years and was made into a box office smash.

But Jack Tyler wasn't finished with unclogging the pipes. He was appointed to the board of seven Fortune 500 companies where he earned valuable stock options, and respect in the business community—for wielding his plumber's snake to the benefit of stockholders.

Tyler eventually grew weary of his popularity and the public attention, so he hung up his tools and retired. He withdrew from society, became a recluse, and never married.

Ellie Sherman wrote in her column:

"I knew lots of single women who would have made a good match, but he told me once that he never got over his flames of passion for Lois Laney."

Postscript

By Timmy Olsen

Long after Jack Tyler left the public stage, I was able to secure a meeting with him. Beforehand, I learned he was a loner who lived with two cats at a Xanadu-like waterfront estate and had refused all contact with the press for several years.

I arrived at Tyler's stately residence one morning at the appointed time. I rang the bell, heard it echo inside, and waited.

After a few minutes, two cats came to the front door. They greeted me and demanded a handout. I didn't have any cat food, so I offered to write a story about their plight. My offer was well received by the cats and they rubbed against my leg.

Then one of the cats pushed open the door to the massive house and led me into a dim hallway.

"Come on back," I heard Tyler call from a distance.

I went to the entrance of a cathedral-like room. It had a black marble floor, columns, and a high ceiling. Two red wingback chairs stood opposite each other at the far end, near a picture window, which was the only source of light.

Jack Tyler was seated on the left with an unlit cigar in his hand. "Please, take a seat," he said.

He was dressed in a blue shirt, black jacket, and black pants. A green tie with tiny Santa figures was loosely knotted around his neck.

I studied his face as I sat and saw the toll taken by the passage of time. He appeared wrinkly, weak, and weary, and had gained weight since I'd last seen him in person, many years ago.

"It's been a long time, Olsen," Tyler said. "Good to see you. You haven't changed a bit since we worked together investigating sewers."

"Thanks, Governor," I said as I pulled out my reporter's notepad and pen. "It was an adventure, however, I didn't do as well as you did—"

He held his hand up, palm facing out, and said, "Please call me Jack, I'm a private citizen now."

"Yes . . . Jack," I said. His command made me nervous so I checked my prepared questions and said, "In spite of many hard knocks and public battles, you look as if you came through in fine shape."

"Well, to tell you the truth, I don't have the fire in my belly anymore and I'm glad it's over." He placed the cigar in his mouth, lit a match, puffed, and turned the stogy to light it. "There were too many ups and downs."

"I'd like to talk about your ride . . . . You have lots of fans who love you because you enjoyed the heat in the kitchen," I said. "Now that you're a private citizen again, I'd like to ask about your first big confrontation when you burst onto the public scene."

He did not respond.

"That time," I continued, "during your first campaign for governor when your former employer published an angry and critical editorial about your qualifications for office."

He nodded for me to continue.

"It's been said that Walker's editorials were the low point in your life. Were they?"

"They sure gave me indigestion," he said. "But they were heaven-sent because they showed Walker's terrible bias."

"Was Walker really biased and unfair to report your attempts at infidelity? . . . After all, the voters loved you for exposing the same foibles of your political opponents."

The old man raised his chin and slowly exhaled.

"Walker was absolutely biased and unfair," he said. "But I was glad he paraded that fisherman's wife, who laughed at my dress and cologne, in front of the public—because it gave me the opportunity to speak to the average Joe.

"I believe what turned the tide is when I did not deny Walker's story, but instead, told the citizens my ties and cologne were all I could afford on a reporter's salary. My candid reaction resonated with the hard-working man and woman—much to the dismay of the privileged ruling elites who think they dominate the political arena."

While I noted his response, Tyler shifted in his chair, as if he was in a bit of discomfort. After I finished writing, I made eye contact and continued.

"Now that you're out of the public eye," I said, "I'd like to get your side of the story as to why Walker fired you."

Tyler flicked the ashes from the cigar into an ashtray, settled into the chair, and took several labored breaths.

"After Walker told me during our sewer story exposé, 'You

don't know shit from shinola,' I decided I'd had enough of his personal bias against me."

"So you quit before he fired you?"

"Yes."

"That's not the story Norton Walker tells."

"Is that old man still breathing?"

"Yes."

"Then I won't speak ill of him, except to say an editor is supposed to remain neutral, fair, and balanced."

"Are you biased against Walker?"

"I tell you I'm not biased against Walker in any way."

"Do you hate Walker?"

Tyler exhaled a puff of smoke and held the cigar off to his right side. I surmised he was impressed with my follow-up question.

"Absolutely not," he said.

"One time, after you left a meeting in Walker's office, he showed me red marks on his neck that he said were caused by your hands. . . . Did you ever try to choke him?"

"That's typical of an editor—re-writing a reporter's copy to change the meaning and slant the news."

"You really didn't answer my question," I said. "Why the red marks on Walker's neck?"

"He was having difficulties with his tie. I merely lent a hand to help him loosen it."

"Really?"

"You know," he said, "I could use this opportunity to smear Walker with a bit of unflattering personal information but I won't stoop to his level and tell you he has ring around the collar."

I knew I was close to obtaining a provocative quote that could be used to drive readers to the story—all I had to do was goad Tyler just a little bit more.

I hesitated and used the pause to think of a trick question.

Finally I said, "I don't understand. . . . What is it about Walker that you like and admire?"

"Nice try, Timmy." The old man smiled. "I admire Editor Walker because he taught me a reporter's job is to find out what makes people angry. At first I didn't understand why anger was so important to the news business, but I quickly learned its amazing power . . . and so I can't be mad at him . . . or express my personal bias that I think he practiced yellow journalism."

"Is there more to the story of your last day at the newspaper?"

"Yes, your journalistic instincts are correct," he said. "There is more. . . . While I argued with Walker about the merits of the newspaper spending six months to produce a statewide sewer exposé, he began yelling the real sewage problem was politics.

"The more he yelled about it, the madder he got. When he reached the peak of madness, I thought he was going to pass out from lack of air. When I tried to remove his tie to help him breathe, he got angry at me for making him so angry."

"Is that when he fired you?"

"No."

"Then why did he say he fired you?"

"Well, I figured since he had worked himself into a tither, I should take advantage of the situation—and put my mind at ease regarding something I was mad about—I told him I was jealous that he was having an affair with Lois Laney."

"Really?"

Tyler's face turned ashen and I wondered if I had pressed him too hard. He took a couple of labored breaths and gripped the armrest of his chair.

"I never had any proof," he said, "and even Lois denied it. So I cannot tell you that Walker had an affair with Lois. It would be wrong to report."

"Okay."

"But let me be crystal clear about something else," he said. "Walker was right about one thing—politics is the real sewer system."

The old man coughed and wheezed. His eyes became glassy and it seemed there was only time for one more question.

"Citizen Jack," I said, "is there anything else you want to add that I haven't asked you?"

The aging, overweight old man coughed again, set his cigar in the ashtray, and fell forward in his chair. In the low voice of a famous actor and former wine salesman, Tyler whispered these final words before he died:

"Please tell Lois she will always be my Rosebud."

Life Flight

We sat in the midnight darkness on cheap but comfortable patio chairs. The kind with thick padding wrapped in vinyl, decorated with yellow and orange spring flowers. Chairs that sit unused in winter, inside the garage, waiting for the warm nights of summer.

But the nights were cooler now and the days shorter. And soon the fireflies would disappear.

She puffed on a cigarette and we said nothing. I studied her lips, which glistened with lip gloss, as they wrapped around the filter. My chair creaked as I shifted my position, and I swallowed more beer to ward off the silence.

A pair of headlights lit up the driveway, the back door opened with haste, and her daughter ran out of the house.

"Mama," she said, "I'm going to get an ice cream with Lisa."

"It's 11:45," she said. "Your curfew is in 15 minutes."

"I know—I'll be home in time."

"Tiffany, don't make me worry."

"I won't—bye."

A car door slammed, the headlights backed away, and the two of us were alone.

The distant sound of a helicopter grew louder. She turned, rocked back in her chair, and looked skyward at the flashing lights.

"Life Flight," she said.

"What?"

"Emergency helicopter going to Metro."

"How do you know?"

"It used to land on the roof of the Akron ER." She studied the lights as it flew away. "Going from Southwest to Metro. Critical patient they can't handle." She took a puff. "Someone will get a dreaded phone call."

"Why can't Southwest handle it?"

"Metro is a Level One Trauma Center."

"What's that?"

"The worst . . . head trauma, spinal injuries . . . gunshots."

"I thought every hospital could handle those?"

She stubbed out her cigarette in the ashtray. "They stabilize and move them to Metro where they have more staff and state-of-the-art equipment."

I watched the helicopter fly beyond the trees and out of sight—the flashing lights warning the guardians of life to prepare for arrival.

"Why move someone? It seems more dangerous than staying put."

"Not if it's serious."

"Isn't that risky . . . and expensive?"

"Look at it this way," she said. "You never know when it will be the last time you see someone. Isn't it best to do everything possible?"

The sound of the helicopter faded into the city noises of distant sirens and freeway traffic. My beer tasted warm and flat, and I smelled the smoke from her cigarette.

"What was the worst you ever saw in the ER?" I said.

After a long wait she answered, "There were too many . . . an eighteen-year-old who shot himself in the head."

"Suicide?"

She shook her head no. "I don't want to discuss it."

I glanced around the back yard and looked at the fence which provided a sense of privacy from outsiders listening to our conversation.

"Why not?" I asked.

"I'm not good with it."

"But I want to understand." Our eyes met. "Remember—you said one day we would be able to tell each other anything."

"This is something I don't want to share. It's hard to discuss children and hospitals. I told you that before."

"Yes, you did." Then, "It's weird, I have an urge to know. Do you think I'm being . . . morbid?"

"It's because you don't understand what it's like to lose a child—you've never been a parent."

"Maybe you can explain it to me?"

She sipped her wine, twice, and set the glass tumbler on the plastic tabletop. "He was playing Russian roulette at home with two friends . . . the night before his high school graduation. His mother heard the gunshot."

My God. I turned my head and stared at the red bricks of the patio.

Then I heard, "The squad did everything they could."

I shook my head side-to-side and clenched my teeth.

She stiffened and spoke in her professional tone, "There was nothing we could do. His mother was distraught when she arrived at the ER. The boy was her only child."

She tapped out a cigarette from the pack on the table, put it to her lips, and flicked a lighter. I saw the color of life in her face as the tobacco glowed.

"I was on the trauma team that met them at the door. We performed CPR for thirty minutes before the doctor called it."

"I don't understand."

"He was dead."

I looked past the fence, into the blackness, and finally said, "I've never heard such a story."

Her eyes wandered and then she looked directly at me. "I told you. It's hard."

I tapped my fingers on my knee and thought about what I could possibly say. Finally I said, "It must be difficult to work in the ER."

"Yes, it is." She looked through me at something she could see but I could not. After a long wait she added, "I don't know if I will ever be able to explain it."

I wondered why I didn't understand.

"Were you afraid?" I said.

"There is no place for fear in the ER. You see the emergency and are focused on saving a life—you must be prepared for anything."

I nodded in agreement.

She puffed, blew smoke up and away, and continued, "You see this kind of stuff and deal with it. . . . When it's over, you sit down—thankful it wasn't your kid—and that's when fear takes hold."

"What do you mean?"

"You're always relieved when the squad comes in and it's nobody you know." She stubbed out her cigarette and pursed her lips. "After it's all over, you think about your own kids . . . then fear seeps into your soul and stays."

"How do you deal with that day in and day out—I mean—with Tiffany?"

"You just do."

"But what about the dreaded phone call?"

"I can't keep her locked up."

We were silent for a long time. I finished my beer and went to the kitchen for another and wished I had brought a sweater to ward off the outdoor chill. Soon it would be time to return the patio chairs to their place inside the garage, protected from the cold and gray.

I heard a siren and then her cell rang.

"Who would call at this hour?" I heard her say.

Tensed, I moved to the door.

"Hello? . . . I can't hear you. . . . Yes. . . . Please be careful."

She looked up to me and smiled, "That was Tiffany—she is bringing us ice cream."

Life On Mars?

NEW YORK CITY—A half-eaten hot dog has been discovered on the surface of Mars. The startling news was presented this morning during the keynote address at the annual Conference of Astronomical Oddities by NASA spokesman John Cameron Swayze.

"Extraordinary claims must be backed by extraordinary evidence," Swayze said. "The discovery of a hot dog on another planet is the first indisputable proof we are not alone."

The news caused the standing room only crowd to gasp loudly, and it eventually led to a riot between the believers and deniers. The audience, composed of scientists, scholars, and specialists, were packed inside the main auditorium for the formal announcement of what some have claimed is humankind's greatest scientific discovery.

"It's way beyond the wheel and way beyond relativity," said attendee Albert Einstein, Theoretical Physicist. "The recent discovery of the Higgs bosen God particle is soooo last year."

Spokesman Swayze explained the outer space weenie and two pieces of a bun were photographed by Mars rover Curiosity, which landed on the surface on August 5, 2012.

"Mars has intrigued scientists, philosophers, and kooks for many generations," Swayze said. "Now we have first-hand evidence their obsession with Mars was justified."

The amazing photographs show the half-eaten mystery meat apparently where it was abandoned. Close-up pictures reveal possible bite marks on the hot dog and the bun. NASA scientists were also intrigued by the possible find of remnants of a Big Gulp cup.

"The remnants have decayed and cannot be conclusively identified," Swayze said. "However, one top NASA scientist believes a portion of the 7-11 logo is visible in one photograph and he theorizes a Big Gulp was discarded along with the hot dog."

Swayze offered no explanation as to how the hot dog and the Big Gulp got to Mars, but he suggested whoever was enjoying them may have had enough.

The announcement of the discovery was met with loud gasps, then stunned silence, and finally cheers from the audience of really smart people dressed in either white lab coats or tweed jackets with elbow patches.

It also led to boos and catcalls from those in attendance who denied NASA's fantastic discovery and challenged the photographic evidence.

"It's outrageous—a hot dog on Mars," said Dr. Jack Diamond, an outspoken NASA critic and a noted conspiracy expert. "The government must be insane to think we would believe this canard."

Diamond is best known as the radio talk-show personality who channels dead U.S. presidents to discuss historical conspiracies. He rose to fame after his live television special which featured pointed questions directed at former President Herbert Hoover about who really invented the vacuum.

The dozens of deniers, led by Diamond, stood in the rear of the auditorium and jeered NASA's announcement. Later, Diamond shouted questions at the scientific panel who took the stage to discuss the findings.

"This is a scam put upon the American public by NASA and the Big Hot Dog industry," Diamond yelled into a megaphone at one point during the proceedings. "NASA wants more Federal funding and Big Hot Dog wants more government largess to line their pockets. They are manufacturing an urgent Martian hot dog crisis to get taxpayer money!"

Diamond went on to yell, "Those government morons are one step away from claiming hot dogs from Mars are unhealthy and a threat to our lifestyle on Earth. The next thing they will say is all Martian hot dogs must be eliminated. Then they'll insist on a hot dog tax to curb demand. We've heard this story all too many times."

The controversy wasn't limited to questions about whether or not Big Hot Dog planted the evidence or whether or not a Martian hot dog diet poses a health hazard.

Chaos erupted after several hot dog specialists on the scientific panel offered competing theories as to what type of hot dog appeared in the photos.

However, among the believers, excitement was feverish as urgent pleas were made to send humans to Mars to bring the artifact back to Earth for further study.

"We absolutely must get it as soon as possible," said astronomer Carl Sagan. "It's a profound discovery that will change our understanding of the Universe—and it will forever alter our knowledge regarding the importance of hot dogs in the evolution of life."

Dr. Sagan, dressed in his signature turtleneck during these times of global warming, went on to say, "It may be that we should search for hot dogs rather than water in our efforts to find life beyond Earth."

NASA spokesman Swayze, and the scientific panel, were unable to pin down the age of the hot dog and bun, or even what kind it was.

Dr. Sagan reacted, "We aren't sure how old the cylindrical meat sausage is. Mars is a cold place, so the mysterious weenie toss could have taken place yesterday—or millions of years ago. We have so few facts about this amazing discovery. Why . . . we don't even know if it's skinless or Chicago style."

Sagan added, "There literally are billions and billions of possibilities as to what form of indigenous life may have left the hot dog at its present location. In any event, the discovery means I must return as host of my show."

Because there is no way to date the age of the discovery without a sample return mission, scientists can only speculate if the wayward weenie was abandoned, tossed, or discarded. Furthermore, NASA's scientific panel offered wildly competing theories as to who or what last touched the hot dog and bun.

Meanwhile, in the back of the auditorium, the unruly and vocal crowd of doubters raised important questions.

"Why are we to believe NASA?" Diamond said. "They can't even tell us what ingredients are in a Martian dog. Nor can they tell us who left it for us to find."

Speculation as to who or what may have last touched the hot dog ran the gamut of possibilities. Some experts said an extinct creature, perhaps a meat-eating Martian dinosaur, was responsible.

Another group of scientists postulated a Martian Dachshund dropped the hot dog after stealing it from an unwary guest at a summertime barbeque.

However, the most controversial theory offered as to how the wayward weenie arrived at its present location involved a toddler, temper tantrum, and sauerkraut.

Dr. Frank Weiner-Mann, world renowned sausage expert, took the side of NASA and made a guess as to the type of hot dog discovered.

"It's about 3 inches long with a regular white bun," Weiner-

Mann said as he studied the extraordinary photo with his one good eye and a jeweler's loupe. "I'm certain it's a Hormel or an Oscar Mayer."

Other specialists in attendance expressed even more startling opinions.

Abu, owner of the Quickie Mart in Springfield where Bart Simpson resides said, "That's a Ballpark Frank. I sell three for 99¢—condiments and buns extra."

Elmo Gelmo, the proprietor of a hot dog stand in front of a home improvement store said, "It's a Hebrew National . . . part of my two dog special."

Dr. Braun Schweiger, a Hungarian refugee and Wiener Specialist, had a different take on the discovery.

"The significance of this being identified as a Hebrew National hot dog will rewrite the Bible," Dr. Schweiger said. "We now have proof the Jewish Exodus from Egypt was far more extensive than originally believed, ranging much further than the deserts of the Middle East."

Unfortunately, none of the experts were able to determine if the fascinating find was a beef, turkey, or corn dog and many unanswered questions lingered, long after riot police cleared the auditorium.

Things got heated, then fiery, when Dr. Sagan pushed his way to the podium and said, "This is a fascinating astronomical mystery. We need to send another probe to Mars to bring back a sample. Only then can we answer fundamental questions about the crowd-pleaser. Was it steamed, boiled, or grilled? And do the Martians prefer their dogs garnished with ketchup, mustard, and relish?"

Sagan's statements triggered an audience free-for-all, led by The Show-Boaters, a group of raunchy scientists dressed in tight pants. The Show-Boaters stormed the stage, seized the microphone, and bragged the Martian find was part of *their* foot-long dog.

The ruckus caused other scientists to vehemently disagree, and blows rained down on various eggheads as they insisted The Show-Boaters only had a cocktail weenie.

Sanity prevailed for a short time, and the groups were separated, after Dr. Sagan pounded the podium with his fist and requested everyone to settle down.

After calm was momentarily restored Sagan said, "The only thing we can all agree on is that it's not a cheese dog."

Then the situation went volcanic after a sect of believers, wearing the tweed jackets with elbow patches, wrestled away Jack Diamond's megaphone and used it to claim NASA may soon discover a Pink's hot dog stand near the mystery weenie and that Earthlings need to prepare for an imminent Martian invasion.

Those claims reignited the angry crowd and soon calls for vengeance were made by scientists who feared the Martian hot dog might be of danger to Earth due to its high concentration of sodium nitrate.

"Based on the evidence presented, it's possible the Martian hot dog eater was a victim of an unhealthy diet," said Dr. Robert Atkins, physician and cardiologist. "Or, it's possible the thin atmosphere on Mars allows Martians to eat hot dogs with high concentrations of carcinogens, making them into Super Martians who will invade Earth and turn us into human hot dogs."

A mob of white lab coats stormed the stage after Atkins yelled, "I will resist all attempts to fund a sample return mission until we have a better understanding of Martian frankfurter safety."

NASA spokesman Swayze tried to hold back the swarming lab coats by claiming rush plans were being drafted to send a Martian probe, dubbed the Weenie Flyer, to search for additional evidence.

Then, dissenting scientists who disagreed with the group trying to take control of the stage, gathered on the left side of the auditorium and chanted, "One More Rover!"

But things went nuclear after Dr. Braun Schweiger stole the podium microphone from Swazye, and over the chants of "One More Rover!," yelled no science could be accomplished with an unmanned Weinermobile.

The lunatic fringe groups gathered in the back of the auditorium became unhinged and tried to drown out the chants of "One More Rover!" by screaming, "Big Government is hiding Martians!"

Then Jack Diamond led his angry protestors toward the stage, while whistling the Oscar Mayer Weiner tune, and forced a confrontation with the band of scientists who controlled the stolen megaphone.

When the two groups met, an enraged Diamond threw himself onto the opposition speaker, took back his megaphone, and shoved several objecting scientists to the ground. Then Diamond made his way to the podium microphone and ranted through his megaphone.

"Mars is a place of war, the difference between men and women, and it has tried to invade Earth," he said. "It has starred in man's imagination as *The Martian Chronicles*, *The War of The Worlds*, and *My Favorite Martian*."

Stunned silence swept the room again as the lab coats and tweed jackets stopped fighting to listen to Diamond shout through the megaphone into the auditorium sound system.

"All of this creative fantasy has a basis in fact," Diamond yelled. "And that fact is the government has concealed the discovery of living Martians since 1976, after the Viking 1 spacecraft photographed the rock formation known as the Face On Mars."

Diamond claimed he funded an intense study, featuring swimwear models using a supercomputer, that determined the Face On Mars had an uncanny resemblance to Yogi Berra.

"The discovery was hushed up by the authorities," Diamond said, "because they couldn't believe Yogi Berra had achieved godly status on Mars!"

Other skeptics, emboldened by Diamond's direct and persuasive challenge, voiced more objections and then made claims the hot dog photo is phoney.

Linq "Ed" Salami, PhD., argued, "Curiosity is not even on Mars. The entire mission has been faked like the Moon landings." He added, "Neil Armstrong was not a real person. He was just made up by fiction writers who worked the government."

Salami then said, "Those supposed Mars rovers are not even on Mars—they're actually inside Yankee stadium."

The mention of New York's favorite team brought former Yankee head honcho George Steinbrenner into the fray. He beamed down, grabbed the podium microphone from Salami, and said, "Is that really a Mars rover on the field? . . . I thought our grounds keepers were testing a robot mower before opening day."

Steinbrenner's sudden appearance from parts unknown caused pandemonium. Riot police were called and some eggheads were cracked before order was restored.

In spite of the vehement disagreement at the formal announcement, if the reports of the half-eaten hot dog and remnants of a Big Gulp are true, the discovery would be of profound significance to humanity.

As a result, it would also be time to rewrite humankind's greatest achievement as: *One small bite for man, one big gulp for mankind.*

Oh, and is their life on Mars? Yes, and we are the Martians.

The Driver

Sara lay awake, her mind churning with troubled thoughts. She glanced at the clock: 2:38 a.m.—four hours until work.

Rick's words echoed again in her mind, *Why did he leave? Why?*

Earlier that morning, Rick sat stiffly at the kitchen table. As she brought him a cup of coffee he said, "Sara, sit down . . ."

"I'm late for a staff meeting," she said. "Can't we talk after I get home?"

"No. It can't wait." He looked past her. "I've got to say it now—my passion is gone. It's not the same any more." Then Rick added, with a voice used to instruct a taxi driver, "I just want us to be friends."

She stopped and her heart raced.

Then: "Please, Rick. Don't do this. Not now."

"I don't want to hurt you, but it's not working. I can't pretend anymore."

"Please don't do this. I love you. I'll do anything . . . please, let's keep trying."

"No. . . . I can't force this. It's over Sara." He pushed back his chair and stood. He sighed and went to the front door of her cramped apartment and left without looking back.

Now, in the dark of night, she was lost and alone and hurt. She was afraid to reach out to anyone, as if held tight by a straight jacket. She told no one at work nor her friends—because she didn't know what to say. Rick did not return her calls, and no matter which way she rolled in bed she couldn't escape the nightmare.

A sadness like oppressive humidity enveloped her. Like this night, hot and sticky. No trade winds to rustle the curtains. No breeze to whisper dreams. Just tropical heat and loneliness.

Why doesn't he want me. . . . Is it really over?. . . No, I don't believe it.

She cried into her pillow which was wet with tears.

Miki, her dog, whined. She looked at her little friend who waited with a wagging tail that said, "I'm here."

The woman stroked his head and scratched his face and chin. Miki licked her hand. Her loyal friend. The glow of the clock announced the passing of another minute.

She looked at the night stand, a garage sale find. It was old and stained and covered with a cloth of yellow-and-blue flowers. Her car keys and purse were next to the clock, and she saw her jeans draped over a white wicker chair in the corner.

It was time to escape. To get as far away as she could. To cry the sadness away in the dark, lonely night.

She remembered her father and how he would leave home when she was a child. Mother was terminally ill and needed constant care. Sometimes Pappa reached his limit and he'd grab his keys and cigarettes and say he was going for a drive to nowhere in particular. He would vanish for hours, leaving her alone with Mother, and return late at night. Pappa never spoke about his feelings, and she bottled all the fears of a five-year-old child, tight, to keep them away.

Sara stood, her tall, slim body casting a dim shadow across the floor. She dressed and slipped on flat, leather sandals. They were comfortable sandals, the ones she preferred, even though they were scuffed and worn.

In the kitchen, lit only by a microwave digital clock, she poured a glass of red wine. She sat at the kitchen table, sipped the wine, and thought about Pappa. He liked to drink French wine. He said it took the edge off and made things easier. She drank another glass of wine and felt mild relief from the sting of loss.

Yes, I'll do like Pappa . . . go for a drive.

Sara gathered her purse and keys and picked up Miki. She opened the front door, made her way down the staircase, and saw the silhouettes of familiar shapes.

She went to her car, a red two-door sports coupe, pressed a button on the key fob, and heard the doors unlock. Miki jumped on the passenger seat as she slid inside and started the engine. She felt light-headed from the wine and did not turn on the headlights—no reason to disturb the neighbors or the landlord.

I'm okay.

Carefully, she backed out of the driveway. Nobody would know she left or her destination. Even she did not know.

Just for a drive, just to get away, just like Pappa.

She drove slowly along the street. After traveling a block, she turned on the headlights—two beacons pushing against the silent darkness that enveloped her.

The road was empty and the houses were dark. The only intrusion was the rumble of the engine. She rolled down the window and let in the night air.

Her dog, her car, and the road ahead. That is all she could see. She reached the stop sign at the end of the road, applied the brakes, and drove onward, wondering what to do.

It was the same question she asked herself many times as she journeyed through life. And no matter where life took her, loneliness always lingered nearby, like a melancholy shadow. She looked faraway along the road and saw the red and white reflection of another stop sign.

Where am I heading . . . should I go back?

She came to the stop. The road branched to three different routes.

She hesitated and turned onto the largest street—the one with streetlights but no moving cars. She shifted into second and then third gear. Driving took some of the hurt away, like ointment on a burn. She let herself cry and did not wipe away the tears.

What is it about me that I can't hold onto a man I love?

This disappointment cut.

Life was a never-ending struggle. She squeezed the steering wheel in frustration.

Why go on?

She shifted into fourth and went faster. Miki laid on the seat. The dog was tired and did not jump against the door to watch the world pass by the window.

I need him. Why didn't he ever say, "I need you?"

He wanted out—the same as every other man she loved and wanted.

If he needed me, he would stay.

If he needed her—the heartfelt words that provide comfort and meaning. Simple words that would mark her place in the world and would ensure she would never be alone.

Instead, there had been generous compliments about her appearance and personality. And friends reassured her that she was a great catch—and she would find *him* any moment. But she didn't feel the confidence in herself to understand Rick was not the one.

The red sports car turned onto a four-lane commuter highway. The main line that carried workers, students, and families to their daily appointments. She saw a few cars, guided by faceless individuals, visible as silhouettes illuminated by the glow of an instrument panel.

She shared an occasional passing glance with these unknown night travelers who were separated by six feet of roadway and the metal of a car. Each driver on a solo journey, moving with the flow of traffic, in the dead of night.

The dead of night. The place of graveyard workers who quietly prepare the city or clean the mess. Silent and efficient, like the workers who ready a corpse for the final resting place.

The driving was easy and she made nearly every light. The red car, Miki, and the woman, passed closed shopping centers, scattered all-night convenience marts, darkened homes, and the shadows of the night. Sometimes they shared the road with another car or two, all traveling the same direction, but not the same destination. She drove away from the city and drove away from her troubles.

The wide, smooth, well lit, four-lane road became a narrow, two-lane drive. A twisting road without street lights. She liked to drive roads like this—where she could go fast, use both hands on the wheel, and do lots of gear shifting.

She let go of her sad thoughts to concentrate on the road—the headlights warning of dangerous curves lurking ahead. She sped up and pushed her car faster. She felt better when adrenaline lifted her spirits as she took a curve. She pressed on the gas and shifted again. She felt in control of the car and pushed against the limits—ready to break through her pain and find relief.

Miki gripped the seat with his claws, but the curves threw the dog off balance. He was scared, but Mama was there and so the squealing noises must be okay.

The narrow road climbed uphill and cut through an ancient lava flow of hard, black rock. The car reached the top of the climb. The road, carved into the side of the mountain, flattened out and twisted parallel to the rocky coast.

To her right, the view opened to the ocean, with a half moon high in the sky. The horizon, a thin, slightly curved line, divided the darkness of the sky and the blackness of the water. Hundreds of feet below, the Pacific Ocean smashed against the ragged shoreline. Huge ocean swells that traveled 2,500 miles unimpeded met the island—surging and crashing endlessly against the black volcanic rock.

A low, white guardrail separated the pavement from a plunge to the water. A thin ribbon between life and death.

She thought about her mother, taken away long ago. How Pappa was lost and alone. How she and Pappa carried on, just the two of them. She thought about Pappa's death, leaving her alone in the world. She thought about how he taught her to drive. How she never liked his smoking. And now, just like Pappa, she smoked because it made things easier.

She went faster, using her driving skills and confidence to keep the car on the twisting road. Twice she felt the rear end of the car slip as she went through a curve. And each time she expertly corrected the steering and kept the red car in the safe zone. Then a third slip.

I've got to slow down.

But she did not.

Rick doesn't care. . . . He doesn't need me.

She remembered his smile. The look in his eyes. The safe feeling he gave her. The warmth of his touch. She began to cry, almost lost control, and felt the rush of adrenaline.

Nobody wants a 46-year-old woman.

The plunging darkness on the right, the unforgiving lava rock wall on the left. Either side, an inviting release. Relief from the torment, relief from the loneliness, relief from the hurt.

Miki is here. We'll go together.

It would be easy to feel in control until physics took them away.

She went faster. The next left curve was the sharpest—a silent free fall to freedom beckoned.

The car went into the curve too fast. She downshifted and braked, trying to slow as she turned the wheel left into the curve. The car was on the right side of the centerline and she could take the turn with more control, if she moved left, across the centerline. But she did not—she stayed on her side of the road.

And then: oncoming headlights crossed the centerline and came straight at her.

Instinctively, she swerved to the right. The shift threw her against the driver's door. Bright lights flashed past. And the little red car careened toward the ribbon of safety. She panicked and slammed the brake pedal. The car slid sideways, out of control, and the ominous sound of screeching tires foretold the outcome.

Maybe it was her survival instinct and quick reactions. Maybe it was Pappa. Maybe it was a higher power. Something took control.

The steering wheel turned right, into the slide, and her foot came off the brake. The red car obeyed and veered away from the death plunge. Sara stayed on this side of the thin, white line. The car stalled and came to a stop.

In the silence, she started to tremble. She gripped the steering wheel with both hands and sobbed, giving in to the pain. Miki jumped into her lap. She sat this way for many heartbeats, shaking and afraid. She fumbled for a cigarette, lit it, and began to calm down. She started the car and put it in gear.

She drove slowly as the fear and shaking ebbed. The road led her to scenic Makapu lookout, five hundred feet above the rocky shore. There were no other cars and no smiling tourists taking pictures and pointing at the scenery.

She looked out to the view—the wide, dark expanse of the Pacific stretched as far as she could see, lit by the soft light from a half moon. A magnificent view, serene and gorgeous.

She felt the trade winds blow against her face and heard the faint crash of the surf. She smoked another cigarette and felt better.

And she watched puffy clouds slowly float past, casting dark, irregular shadows on the surface of the sea. Gentle trade winds nudging the clouds and changing their shape as they moved like mysterious ghost ships on a journey to a destination unknown—guided by a powerful force, distant and unseen.

The puffy clouds drifted, joined, and separated. Some of them grew and merged with others to carry rain to another faraway island. And some of them drifted alone, quiet and peaceful.

She felt better, her adrenaline rush gone. The view was stunning and silent, and she absorbed it for a good long while. Finally, she was ready to go home. She drove down the mountain and came to the curve where she could have been taken away. She stopped and looked at the skid marks which ran near the guardrail.

She put the red car into gear and drove further. She rounded a turn and saw flashing emergency lights.

A shadowy figure waved a flashlight and signaled her to stop. The figure emerged from the darkness and moved close to her car. Through the light of the flares, she saw a twisted gap in the guardrail.

A police officer looked down at her. Officer Kano was a confident, broad-shouldered Hawaiian—his large, strong presence reassuring in an emergency.

"Ma'am, please drive slowly. Stay between the flares."

"What happened?"

"A pickup truck went off the road. Please move along now."

She looked into Officer Kano's eyes and said, "Was anyone hurt?"

"The driver was killed," Kano said. He'd seen people cross the line on many occasions.

She stared at the scene. Dark figures worked by the light of red flares and flashlights that pushed against the darkness. She heard muffled voices and sounds emanating from emergency radios. The good guys, working the graveyard shift, cleaning up the mess. Making things right so the city would be ready for daylight.

Officer Kano spoke softly, "It's time to move along."

Sara felt a lump in her throat and tinge of fear. But this time it was different. The guardrail, the thin white line, twisted and broken, was the cause.

"Yes . . . okay."

The big Hawaiian spoke again, "Be careful, ma'am. Drive safely."

"Yes. . . . Thank you."

Sara looked up to Officer Kano, smiled, and gently pressed the accelerator. The little red car moved slowly and she looked at the broken guardrail.

Then Sara looked beyond the guardrail—to the ocean view, serene and magnificent. And the puffy clouds drifted past, casting night shadows on the surface of the sea.

The Value Of Deception

I usually suffer a case of intestinal discomfort after I learn people have used innuendo, rumors, or lies to soil my good character. This is because I was raised with traditional moral values that required I always speak the truth—sort of like Honest Abe, but without the stovepipe hat.

Unfortunately, I have learned from personal experience that no one *always* speaks the truth. And so, my dear reader, I must propose an unsavory question to you: *Why has deception become so popular?*

Deception arrives, unwanted, at the front door in many forms. For example it can appear as:

Love and achievements listed in obituaries
Ex-spouse Facebook posts
Enhanced drunkard lies spread by men on the prowl
Airline seat size and leg room boasts
Any exclusive invitations offered by direct mail
All exclusive invitations offered by a supermodel
I'd never do that to you hoaxes
Barefaced lies offered during confession
It's not small or tiny doublespeak delusions

Little white lies in kindergarten and then at rest homes
Every tweet from a celebrity
Route advice presented by GPS devices
No . . . I didn't have a vodka smoothie for breakfast.

And the worst kind of deception? *A lie to oneself.*

There are also a good number of professional liars. Among the ones I have encountered:

Craig's list posters and social media junkies
My cat
Criminals, alcoholics, and singles
Fishermen and customer service reps
Weather forecasters and fortune tellers
Politicians, hyenas, and ex-spouses
Book reviewers.

And no list would be complete without mentioning outstanding deceivers Milli Vanilli, Reverend Jim Bakker, and Lance Armstrong.

According to one sage commentator, untruths travel faster than light—which means untruths actually control the speed and expansion of the Universe, negating all good karma I have produced.

Untruths are also a huge industry which I have named Big Untruth. This growing industry is larger than Big Green, Big Oil, and Big Social Media combined. Sadly, Big Untruth influences all aspects of humanity on Earth and anywhere humans might someday congregate.

To prove my thesis about Big Untruth, I offer the example of

Advertising—in all its naked glory, including the infomercial and political propaganda disguised as ads.

As a side note, I would eagerly watch fitness equipment infomercials—if it were mandatory for the "beautiful stars" to shed an item of clothing for each lie presented. I would also enjoy political advertising if the politician were already nude.

In an effort to uncover inside facts about Big Untruth, I contacted celebrity pitchman Ed McMahon for his insight—before his untimely passing. I did this because I believed Ed each year when he promised, "You may already be a millionaire, J. M."

So after throwing away dozens of his invites, I finally accepted Ed at his word and gave up my vow of poverty. I telephoned him to share the good news and to expedite my collection of the pot of gold.

Unfortunately, Ed expressed severe annoyance with me because I had reached him on his home phone—at 3:00 in the morning while he was regaling others about his Conquests of Nookie.

It took Ed a moment to regain his composure after I asked him about collecting my share of the millions.

"Every single fool in America read that promise on the envelope," he said, "and not a single fool has collected."

"But Ed, I'm the first to call you at home, can't I be the winner?"

"Never," Ed barked just before the line went dead.

My entire Ed episode, which includes years of receiving his direct mail solicitations, brings me to this unhappy conclusion:

Marketing and advertising use innuendo, rumors, and lies to convince the gullible, myself included, to buy magazines that are never read and fill shopping carts with useless stuff.

But what value is this to humanity, except to a seller?

In my effort to learn just how humongous Big Untruth is, I then tried to contact O.J. Simpson to better understand why criminals tell the occasional fib.

Unfortunately, I was unable to locate O.J. because he was out looking for the real killer while chillin' in prison. Although disappointed, I pressed onward.

At one time of my life, I was a rabid listener of liberal talk radio. Recollections of this long ago lifestyle reminded me of my fascination with Tush Dimbulb, America's self-appointed Untruth Detector—and appointed by detractors as the No. 1 Rumor-Monger.

As a long-time-ago big fan, I was sure Tush would provide me the straight scoop about Big Untruth.

I showed up at his broadcast studio and received an invite to sit with the Great Orator while he took a ten minute commercial break during his show.

After the formalities were complete, I asked, "Tush, why is politics filled with innuendo, rumors, and lies?"

He blew cigar smoke toward the ceiling and said, "Innuendo, rumors, and outright lies are the way of the political world, my young friend."

"But aren't lies a terrible weapon wielded by bad men?"

"Lies are only a tool—no better or worse than the man telling them. They can be used for good—to grab power, assert control, and make money. Or they can be used for evil—to malign reputations, demonize opponents, and confiscate wealth."

I stared at Tush with wide-open eyes and noticed the countdown clock advancing to the end of the commercial break.

Tush took a puff of his cigar and said, "Before I answer another question, I have one of my own for you."

I nodded yes.

He set the cigar in an ashtray and said, "Would you believe right-wing zealot Helga Klertzman is really Godzilla?"

I was shocked, dumbfounded, and speechless. Finally I said, "I find that hard to believe. . . . conservative Helga Klertzman is Godzilla?"

"Yes, my friend," he said. "It's as true as I am sitting here speaking to you. To prove it . . . have you ever seen Helga in Japan?"

Before I could answer, Tush said, "No! The Japanese won't let her return. They've rebuilt Tokyo too many times." He pounded the table with his fist and added, "You can prove it to yourself—have you ever seen Helga and Godzilla in the same place at the same time?"

I did not respond.

"No!" Tush said. "They never have been seen together. Case closed."

The long commercial break ended and Mr. Dimbulb turned to his microphone. I left the studio and immediately phoned Ms. Klertzman to get her response to Dimbulb's comments.

Her voice message said:

"Help Helga fight the vast left-wing conspiracy. As a supporter, you are invited to join Helga's effort to destroy all liberals, and later, for a Death Match with Rodan."

The voice message ended with this plea:

"Leave your name at the beep and I'll have my people call your people."

I am still waiting for the call.

Since the two giants in the political arena were unable to provide clear insight into deception, I plunged headlong into another vortex of Big Untruth: Male/Female Relationships.

Surely here, I would uncover the value of deception.

Although I can understand the value of common sex lies to the teller, I wasn't sure about the value to a receiver. Sex lies come in many flavors. Popular favorites, which have *never* been spoken to me, include:

You are the best
Size doesn't matter
It's okay, really, sometimes this just happens
The fatal: Let's be friends
I've never been with such a good man
Just this one time, let's go into Victoria's Secret
And, of course, the classic lesbian dissimulation: I did not have sex with that woman.

Sex lies are often bundled with props:

Money clips featuring hundreds
Hair extensions and elevator shoes
Any slimming wardrobe item
Any enhancing costume trinket
Leased sports cars and convertibles
Fashionable leisure suits
Pickles, cucumbers, and bananas
Martinis and umbrella drinks
Thongs or the possibility I might be wearing one.

The sex fable, no matter how outlandish, has many willing accomplices and dupes. This is because "even though there is absolutely no way loser Ralph had sex with that gorgeous woman," men will believe Ralph's assertions because if Ralph got her into bed, so might they.

So, there is lots of value in a sex lie to an individual, but what is the value to society?

I thought to seek the wisdom of a master guru. I expected a long and difficult journey but much to my luck and delight, I found a Magic Swami listed in the Yellow Pages, practicing his craft at an Indian restaurant in Fort Myers.

Because I love the discipline of sitting for long hours at my writing desk, I immediately left to meet with the Magic One even though it was afternoon rush hour.

After a drive of twenty miles, following various elderly who drove aimlessly and slowly, I reached the address of the Magic Swami—a place cleverly named *The Indian Restaurant.*

I parked the Buick and entered. It was dark and dingy inside and the premises smelled like week-old curry. As my eyes became accustomed to the surroundings, I realized I was the only patron in the eatery at the dinner hour.

A small Indian man, named Joe, was the maître d'. I gave Joe the once over and expertly observed he possessed two beady eyes.

He bowed deeply and said, "Welcome, your Highness."

I resisted the urge to make a wise crack about Joe's bald spot because he recognized me as a VIP.

Joe returned to his upright position and said, "We serve only the freshest and tastiest Indian food in Fort Myers. A table for you and the Queen?"

I was once again flattered by his gracious and appropriate greeting honoring my royal heritage, even though the only royal heritage I could claim involved king-size sheets.

"No dinner tonight," I said. "I've come to speak with The Magic Swami."

"The Magic Swami?" he said. "Your highness, do you have an appointment?"

"No, but I have journeyed long and far so that I may speak with him."

Indian Joe frowned and shook his head no. "Swami very busy," he said with a smile. "Cannot see you today."

I figured Indian Joe was lying because, after all, the Yellow Pages advertisement indicated no appointment necessary.

Since I had spent two hours fighting heavy traffic, I was not going to be denied a meet with the Magic Swami by a smarmy, shifty-eyed gatekeeper. It was time to employ all of my royal heritage and the best lie I could invent.

"This is an emergency, Joe," I said. "My head will explode if I don't get to see The Magic Swami—now."

Joe shook his head no and waved the menus he held in his hand.

"If you get me in to see Swami," I said, "I will order everything you serve and pay cash."

Indian Joe arched his eyebrows as he realized he could sell all of his old food, cooked during the week, to an unsuspecting member of royalty. No doubt it was too good to be true.

He motioned me to follow and then he led me through the dining room filled with empty tables. We came to a door marked *Men's*, and entered, and then we went through another door marked *Kitchen*.

He led me through the kitchen, advising me to avoid the spilled food on the floor. Two men, of foreign origin, sat at a table playing cards. We went to another door marked *Authorized Personnel Only*. Indian Joe opened the door, stood aside, and motioned for me to enter.

It was a tiny room with a tile floor, lit by the glow of a single candle. The walls were covered with peeling paint. A low table, in the center of the room, held a burning incense stick.

A bald man wearing an orange robe was seated on the floor, in a cross-legged yoga position. He smiled and motioned for me to sit across from him.

The man looked ageless. He was calm, clean-shaven, and appeared to be full of ancient wisdom. Maybe, just maybe, this

Magic Swami would have the answer I so desperately desired.

"Welcome, Grasshopper," Magic Swami said. "Why have you journeyed so far to visit me?"

I looked into his serene eyes and noticed he resembled Indian Joe.

"I have come seeking the truth," I said. "Why is it that people spread innuendo?"

Swami hinted a smile. "People use innuendo to communicate what they mean without having to say it. This way they can deny what has been said. And yet . . . they have said it," he said. "Like a yin and yang."

I nodded my understanding. Then I detected a whiff of a foul scent. I wondered if the Swami smelled it too.

"Magic One, I am confused," I said. "Why do people spread rumors?"

"People always gossip. Some are motor-mouths," he replied. Then he resumed his serene gaze into space. After a lengthy pause, he spoke. "This is because humans have emotions that give them irrational thoughts. It is normal behavior. People spread rumors so they can embarrass and humiliate others for their own gain. . . . It makes them feel good."

Yes, I nodded.

The foul smell grew stronger and identifiable. I was certain the smell did not emanate from me, although the bean burrito I had eaten for breakfast was suspect. I forgot about my teacher-student dialogue and wondered how to handle the sensitive situation without insulting the Master-Of-All-That-Is-Known.

I chose to ignore the odor and continue my interrogation. "Why, Magic Swami, why do people lie?"

There was a long silence and I heard the faint sound of paint peeling. The tear-forming odor Swami and I now breathed was almost unbearable, and it took every lie I could summon not to comment on the stench.

Swami was unaffected.

"People tell lies for money, sex, or both," he said. "People want money and need sex. They are willing to lie to obtain gratification." He turned his head and crinkled his nose. "That is not to say the pursuit of money or sex is wrong—it just leads to the temptation to lie. Sadly, many people believe the benefits of a lie outweigh the risk—that is why I, Magic Swami, took a vow of poverty and celibacy."

The smell caused tears to run down my cheeks. However, the master was sharing so I avoided any suggestion I was uncomfortable.

Finally, after a long wait, Magic Swami spoke again, "My son, people also lie to escape responsibility and consequences. No one wants to accept blame. Everyone lies. It's the way of the world."

Swami took a deep breath and continued, "Lies allow one to escape embarrassment and humiliation. They are told when one does not know what to say."

A shred of paint peeled away from the ceiling, floated down, and landed on Swami's bald head. He casually brushed it away.

Then Magic Swami wiped a tear from his eye, rubbed his nose, and said, "By the way, it's not from me."

I stared at him in disbelief. There was no question in my mind who was responsible for passing the unpleasant odor. There were no vents in the room, the door was tightly closed, and I knew it wasn't from me.

Swami realized I didn't buy his lame denial and he blushed. Then without warning, he disappeared in a whiff of smoke and I was alone.

I meditated on Swami's words of wisdom and then applied the smell test to his counsel.

Was Swami correct? . . . Does all deception stem from

humankind's basic instincts—the desire for money and the desire for sex?

Yes.

Spreading innuendo, rumors, or outright lies are natural behaviors, which developed during evolution. They are necessary, and valuable, so we can get along in the real world. However, good judgment is required to know when they are acceptable, when appropriate, and how to spot them.

Yes, The Magic Swami was right—they are the way of the world.

I stood and left the room. I retraced my steps through the kitchen and men's room and re-entered the empty dining area.

A smiling Indian Joe waited by the front door and I noticed his beady eyes were watery. He handed me an invoice and several to-go bags.

I stuffed the invoice into my pocket, ignored the bags of food, and said, "I'll put a check in the mail, Joe. . . . Real soon now."

Johnny B. Awesome

John burst into the house and took the basement stairs two at a time. He rushed past his mother, who worked at the washing machine, turned into his room, and saw it was clean.

"Where's my jeans?" he yelled.

"I just put them in the dryer," she said.

"I had a lottery ticket in the pocket—did you take it out?"

"No—"

John pushed past her and opened the dryer door. He grabbed the wet jeans, shoved his hand into the left pocket, and felt the heart-breaking pulp that was a lottery ticket.

He exhaled a howl of devastation. Then: "How could you Mom?" as he hurled the dripping jeans against the far wall.

"I didn't check—"

"I can't believe it—my numbers were picked last night."

"Oh my goodness—I'm sorry."

And that is how John discovered his winning ticket, played with his favorite numbers, was forever gone.

A ticket possibly worth a cool million—spewed by a machine—handled by a convenience store clerk—and casually washed away.

It was the ultimate bummer, in a lifetime of bummers, for appliance parts salesman John B. Grantwood of Cleveland, Ohio.

John called his buddy Tom, who also lived at home with his parents.

"She washed it," he said.

"No way."

"Yes way, dude—destroyed."

"Man . . . that's a jumbo jet bummer."

Neither man spoke for several moments. Finally:

"Dude," Tom said, "let's go to the store. They know you play the same numbers every week. Maybe they got security camera footage, or something."

So off they went.

"I bought the winner here last night," John said.

"Lots of people say they do," the unshaven clerk replied.

"I gave you a twenty. Bought the ticket and a pack of Marlboro Lights."

"Lots of people use twenties, buy cigarettes." The clerk's eyes scanned the store. "It's not my job to remember who buys what."

John pointed at the security camera on the wall behind the cash register. "The camera does."

"It doesn't work."

"What do you mean?"

"I told you. It doesn't work."

John showed the clerk a plastic bag that contained the mushy remains. "This was it—you gotta help me."

The clerk, a lifer at the store, ignored the display.

"I'll give you some if you help prove I bought it."

"How much?"

"25%."

The clerk laughed. "You'll give me 25%?"

"Yeah, of course."

"Your dirty laundry is not my problem—besides, you didn't buy the winner—did you pick the Magic 8 Ball too?"

"Shit, man." John felt a rising tide of panic. "I've played the same numbers every week—and they were picked—I should be the winner."

"Did you have the Magic 8 Ball?"

"Sure I had the Magic 8 Ball." John's throat tightened. "It had to be."

"You're a loser, my friend," the clerk said. "TV just showed the guy who won the jackpot." The clerk tugged at the front of his bowling shirt and said, "Next in line."

John swallowed hard and turned away, his eyes moist. He lowered his head, made his way to the exit, and pushed open the door. As he walked to Tom's car, John B. Grantwood realized he was consigned forever to live in a house owned by his mother.

Over the years, John formed the belief the "fickle finger of fate" was, in reality, an extended middle finger. A finger that sent him a daily, personalized message from the great beyond—a message that said the Giant Wheel of Misfortune pointed to his name, again.

And so, all his adult life, John believed he would *never* win the heart of a pretty girl, achieve success at a high-paying career, or enjoy drinks from the punch bowl at the Dance of Pleasure.

He was a timid and ordinary man who had never traveled more than two hours from Cleveland because travel was fraught with peril—lost wallets, car breakdowns, or upon his return, greetings from Mom that included, "The basement toilet is clogged."

On the evening of the lost ticket, John sat alone on the rear porch, playing the swat-escape game with a house fly.

The house fly was named Fred, after John's elderly boss at the appliance parts store. Fred was an old insect with a bent wing—earned in the struggle to escape a spider's web.

John sipped his second beer and smoked his second cigarette and tried to shake the pain.

Fred buzzed around and occasionally landed on John's person. Each time Fred landed, John made a swat to discourage the tormentor from tickling his skin.

John's surliness bothered Fred, so he landed on top of the open beer can and strutted around where John's lips searched for a swallow.

Fred's unsanitary behavior, although acceptable in the fly world, was unacceptable. John flicked his hand to dissuade the bugger.

Fred flew away, slowly, and landed on the right ear of Mr. Surly.

John, convinced he could end it all for his tiny tormenter, slapped his open palm against the side of his head.

Fred flew into the darkness.

John winced, heard ringing, and said to himself, "Figures."

Mr. Tormentor landed on a wall and watched, through his fly eyes, hundreds of Mr. Surlys.

John thought about the one life he had lived.

Next door, on the other side of the privacy fence, a five-year-old boy laughed and giggled as he played.

The boy's mother called out, "Johnny!"

Fred took to the air and landed on the closest naked forearm.

John made a half-hearted swat.

Fred took off and landed on the other arm.

Mr. Surly cupped his hand and moved it close to Mr. Tormentor.

Elderly Fred, convinced he still had fly mojo, paid no attention to the hand.

John swooped, Fred tried to take off, and the cupped hand closed.

Mr. Tormentor met the same pulpy fate as the lottery ticket.

The young mother called a second time, "Johnny!"

And Mr. Surly was called back to his youth.

That time in life when he rode a Big Wheel and his name was Johnny. When snow was for sledding and throwing and making snow angels. When fireflies were chased and marshmallows were roasted.

When a kid named Johnny raced his bike along the sidewalk on a grand adventure. When he awaited Christmas with eyes that couldn't sleep. When he climbed trees, ran fastest, and caught catfish on a lazy summer afternoon.

That time when he was known as Johnny—before he demanded the world call him by the grown-up name: John.

John took another swig of beer and it suddenly became crystal clear his life went south during adolescence—when he shed his Johnny super hero costume—and donned the heavy John overcoat.

Now, 22 years later, he realized the only time he'd been happy was when he was known as Johnny. And so he vowed on the spot, to change his name back to Johnny.

Beer goggles then produced the idea he should go beyond changing his first name—because his last name, Grantwood, was also a bummer.

A second fly buzzed around, unaware of Fred's fate. This fly also landed on the open beer can. The new Johnny watched the fly and gave it the name George, after a grade school bully.

George left the beer can and alighted on Johnny's knee.

The cupped hand moved into position.

George remained calm and cleaned his wings.

The hand closed the gap.

George sensed the shadow and took flight.

The hand closed around George's world.

Johnny opened his fist, found George's remains, and thought: "That's two in a row—so Grantwood must go."

Johnny did not have any last name replacement ideas—but he was two for two with dead flies and shouts from a young mother. So, being a believer in "Numer-astro-legume-ology," Johnny decided he would change his last name to the first word he heard twice-in-a-row.

He was out of beer, so he walked to the convenience store, intending to resupply the liquid fueling his creativity. It was just past 10 p.m. when he arrived.

He saw two teenage toughs, with tattooed arms, piercings, and dressed in torn jeans and T-shirts. They loitered near a car, in a dark area of the parking lot.

The old John B. Grantwood would have taken a longer route to avoid contact—but the beer-laden, new Johnny squared his shoulders, picked up his pace, and took a direct route past the teens.

"You gotta light?" the bigger tough said.

Johnny stopped, pulled out his lighter, and replied, "Yeah."

Both toughs moved closer.

Johnny flinched but he did not step backward.

"Hey man," the bigger one said as he flashed a $20. "Buy us a 12-pack?"

"What kind?"

"Corona."

Johnny took the bill and nodded.

The toughs smiled and simultaneously said, "Awesome!"

And that is how John B. Grantwood became Johnny B. Awesome.

The next morning Johnny B. Awesome took fate into his own hands. He quit his job as an appliance parts salesman, packed his rusty, two-door Toyota with prized belongings, kissed Mom goodbye on both cheeks, and left Cleveland—on a one-way journey to Las Vegas where his fortune patiently waited.

As the sun set on the first day's drive, Johnny found himself somewhere west of Des Moines on the Interstate. Traffic was light and the driving was easy.

A dirty and dented white Hyundai, with a female driver and a young girl in the passenger seat, sped past, traveling in the fast lane. Johnny exchanged glances with the young girl and watched the car zoom ahead, late for its rendevous.

Suddenly, the Hyundai's right rear tire blew out, scattering debris onto the roadway as smoke poured from the wheel well. The car braked, veered across the lanes, and pulled to the side of the road.

Johnny hit the brakes and gave the Hyundai room to maneuver. As he passed the slowing car, he glanced at the driver—a woman in her thirties.

He thought: *I can't do anything for them—they must have a cell.*

And then Johnny did something he had never done—he braked hard, pulled off the road, and backed up to the disabled vehicle. Then he got out of the Toyota—wanting to help.

But he didn't know why.

When he reached the woman's car, she lowered her window just enough to talk.

"Are you okay?" he said.

"We're all right." Her hands were shaking and her voice cracked as she added, "I should have listened to my mechanic and bought new tires."

Johnny glanced at the passenger, a girl of 8 or 9, and said, "Is she your daughter?"

"Yes."

The woman, who had long dark hair pulled into a pony tail, started to cry. She took a deep breath and regained her composure.

"I can change your tire—"

"I don't have a spare. It's already on." She wiped her eyes with a tissue, looked at her daughter, and then back to Johnny. "We're on our way to see my mother."

"Do you have Triple A?"

"Yes, but. . . . May I use your phone? I don't have a car charger."

"Sure."

Johnny slipped his cell phone through the open window.

Soon a tow truck was dispatched. As she handed the cell back she said, "Thank you . . . they say it'll be 30 to 45 minutes."

"It's getting dark," he said. "Maybe I should stay with you until they arrive?"

"That would be nice . . . but would you mind if I asked you to stay in your car? I would feel more comfortable."

"Yeah, sure. I don't mind." A tractor-trailer passed and its wind rocked the Hyundai. "You don't have to worry, I'll wait until help arrives." He looked to the young girl. "My name is Johnny. You are going to be all right, I promise."

The young girl looked away.

Then he heard the mother say, "We'll be okay, honey." She turned to Johnny and said, "I'm Julie and this is Tamara. We're on our way to Denver—my mother was in a car accident and we've got to get there tonight."

"Don't worry," he said, "they'll get you back on the road and you'll make it." Johnny walked to his car, got in, and waited.

It was dark when the tow truck arrived, with flashing emergency lights. Johnny approached the truck driver and Julie, who were standing by the side of the road.

"Can you help her?" Johnny said.

"She's gonna need a tow and a tire," the tow truck driver said. "I can't fix it out here."

"How much is a tire?" Julie asked.

"About $150."

"I don't have enough money," she said. "I've only got enough for gas to get to Denver. Can I send it to you?"

"No ma'am," the driver said. "I'd lose my job. We take checks and credit cards but my boss would fire me if I gave someone credit."

Julie held back tears. Then she said, "I don't have a bank account or a credit card—I recently filed bankruptcy—I promise I'll send you the money as soon as I get to my mother's house."

"I can't do that," the driver said. "I'll get your car off the road and take you to a motel, but I can't do anything else."

Tears ran down Julie's cheeks when she said, "I don't have money for a motel."

And then, for the second time, Johnny did something the old John would have never done—he opened his wallet and pulled out $200 in cash. He gave it to the tow truck driver and said, "Will this get her back on the road?"

"Yes," the driver replied with a surprised look on his face.

Julie started to protest but stopped.

Johnny turned to her. "I want you to have a safe trip to see your mother. Be careful."

She wiped away her tears and hugged Johnny. "Thank you so much. I'll pay you back when I get the money—I promise."

"No, you don't need to pay it back," he said as he stepped away.

"Wait . . . I need your address."

"No, I want you to have a safe trip." He waved at the young girl inside the car. As he walked further he looked back at the tow truck driver and called out, "Take good care of her."

Then Johnny got into his Toyota and drove onward through the night—feeling odd, maybe even happy.

————

As he drove through the sunrise and into the next day, Johnny fantasized about the perks of his new identity—and the raised eyebrows, smiles, and quips that would be his to enjoy.

If he were paged, he'd hear: "Mr. Awesome, Mr. Johnny Awesome, pick up the courtesy telephone, please."

From a maitre d': "Yes, Mr. Awesome, table for two. Right this way."

And, best of all: "Dr. Awesome, you're needed in the ER."

The Un-Dr. Awesome was sweaty and tired when he arrived in Vegas because the a/c in his aging Toyota had given out just after he passed through Omaha.

He went inside the nearest fancy casino to cool off and give lady luck a whirl on the slot machines. Unfortunately, the slot machines inside the second fancy casino were also unaware of his new identity and the money pile dwindled.

However, there was some good news: the a/c hummed in both locations and Johnny B. Awesome was cool.

It was 3:00 a.m. when Johnny quit his gaming sessions and returned to his car to search for cheap lodging. He drove until he saw a flashing neon sign that read: *Rooms From $19.*

He parked in a lot where the rusty Toyota felt at home, went through a squeaky door, and leaned on a worn-out Formica counter.

"I'd like to get a room for $19," he said to the unshaven clerk, who wore a smelly bowling shirt and resembled the clerk back in Cleveland.

"We don't have any left."

"That's false advertising—the sign says you have vacancies." Johnny B. Awesome made a fist and added, "Will I have to report you?"

"I didn't have time to change the sign," the clerk said. "Only one room available—regular $79—but I will give it to you for $49." He placed a blank registration form on the counter.

An exhausted Johnny shook his head, filled out the form, and said, "I'll pay cash."

"I need to see some ID."

"Why?"

"If you want a room, I need identification."

Johnny fished out his billfold and produced a driver's license.

The clerk eyeballed it and handed it back to Johnny. "I can't rent you the room."

"And why the hell not?"

"False advertising." The clerk chuckled. "You're not Johnny B. Awesome—your license says John B. Grantwood—I don't have to rent you a room—get out of here."

Johnny found a second motel and parked the Toyota. He took a $79 room, registered with his real name, and slept soundly throughout the entire day, waking only twice to use the bathroom.

He dreamt about his streak of two's—including the casinos, the motels, and the need to make an official, permanent name change.

While shaving that evening, he remembered an all-night court house he'd seen while searching for a motel. It was a court house with a neon sign that flashed: *Instant Marriage, Divorce, Bankruptcy, and Name Changes.*

Judge Able Justice, a crusty court veteran, had seen it all and had a few questions for the man who stood before him.

"So," Judge Justice said from up high behind the bench, "you have petitioned my court for a formal name change."

"Yes, Your Honor."

"Johnny B. Awesome—do I have that right?"

"Yes, sir."

"That's an unusual request—and I've seen plenty." A law clerk handed the judge a file folder. The judge opened the folder and reviewed the contents. "My courtroom is sanctioned by the state and I've been a judge for nearly 40 years, so I warn you—do not attempt to fool me."

Johnny leaned toward the microphone and said, "No, sir. I wouldn't dare."

The judge scowled and said, "My law clerk has checked the public records. Are you aware Johnny Awesome is used by singers, comedians, and is a character in a video game?"

Johnny gulped and said, "Do they use the initial B?"

"No."

"Well, Your Honor, then my name is different and I'll give it my own personality, kinda like an impersonator of Elvis."

Judge Justice leaned back in his black leather chair, adjusted his robes, and said, "So you want to be a lounge singer?"

"No, sir. I can't sing and I don't own a tux."

"Good," the judge mused. "We don't need any more around here." The judge sipped a vodka martini—a double. Then he said, "Do you ever expect to ask this court to marry you to Mrs. Awesome?"

Johnny gulped again. "I hadn't thought about finding a girl." Then he displayed a rare moment of glibness. "But it would be awesome."

A trace of a smile appeared on the judge's face and he sipped his martini. Then he said, "Why do you want to change your name?"

"Because my old one does not work. I've got to change my life because—"

"Do you believe a do-over will improve your lot in life?"

"Your Honor, you've got to know when to fold 'em. It's time for me to fold John B. Grantwood."

Judge Justice, a long-time poker player, tapped the gavel and said, "Petition granted." Then he tapped the gavel a second time and added, "If you find Mrs. Awesome, come back—I'll give you my two-for-one special. Case closed."

Three days after officially becoming Johnny B. Awesome, he was nearly broke, dejected, and alone. He pawned his last asset, the Toyota, to increase his measly grubstake—and knew that if he didn't hit pay dirt—he'd be forced to ask Mom to wire money for a bus ticket home.

After stuffing the Toyota cash into his pocket, Johnny took a long walk up-and-down the Las Vegas Strip. He thought about his options and also spoke with the Lord.

Shortly thereafter, Johnny crossed over Las Vegas Boulevard on an elevated walkway above the road. He passed clumps of dirty homeless men, who sat in hungry silence with signs announcing their troubles.

The last homeless man on the walkway, dressed in dirty military fatigues, appeared to be asleep. He held a cardboard sign that read: *Please help. Vietnam Veteran. Homeless and Alone.*

Johnny reached the end of the walkway and went down the stairs. When he got to the sidewalk, he turned around and doubled back to the upper walkway.

And then, for a reason he could not explain, he went to the homeless vet and put $20 into his paper cup.

The vet gave Johnny a vacant stare and said, "Good luck and God bless you."

Johnny went on his way, not sure at all why he chose to help the man, but feeling a bit better.

After wandering in the hot sunshine for hours, Johnny became painfully aware the sand in the timer was low. He was still without a plan and he dreaded what Mom and Tom would say upon his return to Cleveland.

He was tired, so he set off to find his motel. He cut through strip malls, took a construction vehicle roadway, and jaywalked through parking lots. He crossed streets and passed smelly Dumpsters.

After a long walk, he came to a rarely traveled side street and saw the familiar sign of his motel one block in the distance. He continued toward his destination and came across a sidewalk sign.

It read: *Make Awesome Fortune—Secret Blackjack Strategies—2nd Floor.*

Johnny, still without a plan, climbed two flights of stairs and rapped on a locked door. An old Asian man appeared, dressed in a tuxedo. He wore a name tag with his American name and home country. It read: *Johnny Awesome—Korea.*

The young man stuck out his hand and said, "My name is Johnny Awesome, too. I saw your sign."

The old man gently shook hands and smiled. "It is a good name, isn't it?"

"I'm not so sure . . . I've nearly lost all my money . . . I don't think it works."

"I, too, have wondered at times," the old man said. "But I will keep it. . . . Please come inside." He led Johnny into a disheveled office, locked the door, and added, "Just in case someone I don't wish to see comes for a visit."

Inside the cramped, windowless office was a Blackjack table, strewn with playing cards and gambling chips. Two wooden stools—for the player and for the dealer—were on either side of the gaming table. Behind the table was a bookcase, filled with countless boxes of playing cards in their original wrappers.

In a corner, and partially behind a rickety privacy screen, was a desk, covered with Vegas tourist magazines and racing forms. Several faded travel posters of Korean landmarks adorned the walls, all inside metal frames with no glass.

"How did you get the name Johnny Awesome?" the younger man said.

"My stage name," the old man replied. "I was a lounge singer at The Sands for 22 years." He led the younger Johnny to the Blackjack table and waved for him to take a seat on the stool. "I loved to sing Sinatra tunes."

"Do you still perform?"

"No, the hotel was closed and demolished—and after playing there all those years, I couldn't go somewhere else. So I started a second career at the tables—but I was too successful, and too well-known. Now I'm banned from all casinos."

The old Johnny, with practiced hands, shuffled a new deck of playing cards. "Now, please tell me, why did you climb those stairs?"

"I'm desperate—I need the secret strategy."

"How desperate?"

"Extremely."

Old Johnny stopped shuffling the cards and studied the younger man. Then he said, "Desperate men do not make good students."

"I promise to be a good student."

"Can you pay the tuition?"

"After I win, I'll come back to pay you."

"Why should I agree to that deal?"

Young Johnny glanced around the room and looked at the cluttered desk. Then he said, "I can offer you no reason—except my promise to pay you from my winnings."

The old man nodded and said, "To be a good student, you've got to believe."

"I believe . . . you can test me."

"You've already been tested."

"What?"

"Young mother, homeless vet."

"How in the world would you know that?"

The old man did not answer the question. After a pause he said, "I can teach you to play but I cannot teach you to win."

"But . . . how did you know about the young mother?"

"If you want to learn, there will be no more questions."

"So you'll help me?"

The old Johnny Awesome dealt a hand of Blackjack and did not reply.

They played cards for many hours. The veteran explained the nuances of the game and the importance of keeping a vigilant eye on the cards played. Slowly the student became proficient, skilled, and confident at playing the game.

Finally the old Johnny said, "You are ready as you can be. Stay calm and remember you are never alone—I will always be there."

"How do I know it will work?"

"You must have faith. Now it's time to go." The old man led his student to the door and opened it to the sunshine.

Johnny stepped outside, heard the door close, and went down the stairs. He reached the street and noticed the sidewalk sign was gone. Then he looked up to the second floor office and was blinded by the bright sun.

Johnny returned to his motel room and slept for the rest of the day. After he awoke, he felt relaxed and ready to play cards. He went to a fancy casino, made his way to the gaming section, and sat at a Blackjack table with three other players.

The full-breasted dealer welcomed him and cash was exchanged for chips. His heart raced as he placed the minimum bet.

The dealer dealt the new player a King of Hearts—then—an Ace of Spades.

"Blackjack," she said. Her bosom heaved and she smiled as she moved chips toward the player.

Johnny let it ride.

The cards were dealt from the shoe and the house busted. More chips came Johnny's way. His palms were sweaty but he let his winnings ride again and he beat the dealer with two face cards.

The stack of chips grew.

A pit boss hovered in the background.

"Place your bets," the dealer announced.

Johnny pulled his chips from the betting square and placed the minimum bet.

The cards flashed—the dealer won—and they played on.

After many hands, Johnny made another large bet and won.

The pit boss ordered new cards.

And Johnny won again.

As play continued, a crowd grew and cheered when the cards went Johnny's way.

The pit boss waved for a new dealer.

Johnny kept winning.

Finally, the pit boss closed the table.

So Johnny went to another table, placed bets, and the pile of chips grew. So did the crowd. Soon a sultry woman worked her way close and stood to Johnny's right.

He ignored the crowd, the woman, and the offers for free drinks. He remained calm and focused, thought about his mentor, and kept winning.

A muscular man took an empty seat at the table. He wore a tight-fitted T-shirt that had a graphic of a Magic 8 Ball, displaying the message: *Definitely No.*

Magic 8 Ball made bets that matched Johnny's for many rounds, but he lost most hands to the dealer. After he exhausted his funds, Magic 8 Ball joined the crowd that had gathered to watch.

Johnny had played for hours and amassed a large stack of chips.

But like many winning streaks, it ended.

Two large men, with crew cuts and dressed in suits, arrived at the table. They took positions on either side of Johnny and the pit boss announced the table was closed.

Then he turned to Johnny and said, "You're no longer welcome. Take your winnings and leave."

"Why?"

"Acting with intent to defraud a casino."

"What?"

"Card counting."

"I'm not card counting . . . it's lady luck."

The pit boss grimaced. "Consider yourself lucky that we'll let you go." He motioned to the crew cuts.

One of the crew cuts gripped Johnny's shoulder and said, "We'll escort you to the cashier and then outside." He squeezed tighter, causing Johnny to wince, and added, "After that pal, you're on your own."

The chips were gathered and the three men went to see the lady cashier. Johnny bought a nylon sport bag and instructed her to put the dozens of thick wads of $100 bills into the bag. When the cashier was done, she handed him a full bag, and he was escorted to the main entrance.

"I wouldn't enter any other casino," the bigger crew cut said as he shoved Johnny out the door. "Your picture is all over town."

It was 5:00 a.m. when Johnny found himself on the sidewalk outside the casino. He pulled his bag of money close, brushed off the dust, and moved away quickly, blending into the late night crowd.

As he walked along and took stock of the evening, he wondered what next to do. After a short time, he came to the elevated walkway and remembered the homeless vet. He climbed the stairs and found the man in the same location, asleep on a piece of cardboard.

Johnny carefully removed a wad of cash from his bag and placed it in the paper cup.

The vet woke up. He felt the weight of the money, put it into his pocket, and offered his hand. Then the vet said, "God bless you, Johnny B. Awesome."

Johnny left and saw, not too far away, a neon sign for the 24-hour pawn shop that held the Toyota. He hurried down the stairs to street level on his way to get his car.

The crowds thinned as he walked. A car drove by, slowed down, and sped away. Soon, he was only two blocks from the pawn shop—except he had to travel along a darkened side street to reach the bright lights of safety.

He pulled his bag tight and quickened his pace.

From the shadows on Johnny's right, there was movement—then a large man matched his stride. He heard footsteps and glanced over his shoulder. He saw a second big man, wearing a Magic 8 Ball T-shirt.

"Hey buddy," Magic 8 Ball called out. "Got a light?"

Johnny didn't respond and thought to run.

Before he could, a strong hand grabbed Johnny's arm and turned him around. Another hand produced a knife and Magic 8 Ball stood in front of him.

"I know you," Magic 8 Ball said. "You're that real lucky guy." Johnny felt his spittle and heard, "What you got in the bag?"

The cards had been dealt—and Johnny faced two choices: fight or run. He looked toward Providence, said a prayer, and saw a pair of headlights.

The knife disappeared, the hand let go, and the car went past without incident.

Darkness returned.

Then Johnny B. Awesome, facing the fight of his life, saw a second pair of headlights. He took two fast steps to the curb and stuck out his thumb.

The driver was Kylie Sweet, an exotic dancer, on her way home after a long night's work. Ms. Sweet, a Vegas veteran like the judge, had seen it all, especially the behavior of pigs.

It was pig behavior that was the reason Ms. Sweet had never found a man to her liking. And it was also why she grit her teeth when she witnessed the two-on-one full court press.

She braked to a stop near the curb, pulled a handgun she carried for safety, and pressed the switch to roll down the passenger window.

Ms. Sweet pointed the gun at Magic 8 Ball and said to Johnny, "Need a ride?"

Johnny reached for the door handle and his eyes met Kylie's.

For a long magical second, they lingered . . . together.

"You're from heaven," Johnny said. "I'll go anywhere you wish."

And that is how Awesome met Sweet and lived happily ever after.

Dr. Chopstick

or: How I Learned to Stop Buying and Love the Chinese

Warning: For professional use only. Do not try this at home. This story is intended for well-adjusted people with a sense of humor and is not for the faint of heart. If you can be offended in any way, do not read. Put this down immediately and seek counseling. No Chinese were injured in the production of this material.

However, my Siamese cat and Dr. Strangelove refused to speak with me for several days.

Composed in 2006, long before the actual take-over of the world by the Chinese.

In a windowless Situation Room, inside a concrete bunker, buried deep underneath a trailer park, located near Washington, D.C., several really important people held a top secret meeting—and I was invited.

Inside, on the main wall, was a flat screen almost as large as the one in my favorite sports bar. It displayed a map of China, colored in red. Another big screen, on the right side, displayed a map of the United States with hundreds of flashing red dots. And ominously, a large digital sign flashed DEFCON 4 in bright yellow letters.

Several burly men, dressed in military uniforms, worked at fancy touchscreens, pointing, tapping, and swiping.

The President and numerous policy makers were gathered around a long, rectangular conference table in the center of room. The mood was grim and also really serious.

The conference table participants were a stereotypical celebration of diversity. They included two black men, four old white guys, a Native American, two white women, a black woman, a gay and lesbian, two Hispanics, and a guy in a wheelchair who held a pair of chopsticks and who also suspiciously resembled an evil Chinese madman.

The President: This is an absolute crisis. In fact, it may be an off-the-chart crisis and should be re-named a crisis crisis. The situation is untenable and we must have a plan of action. I'll begin with a situation analysis. Go ahead Homeland Security.

Hulkster Hoganhero, Minister of Homeland Security: Sir, millions of Chinese are fleeing China and coming here. Hordes of them. Like a fire drill run amok. On bicycles, motor scooters, rickshaws, and even driving cheap Chinese automobiles. Swarms of black-haired look-a-likes.

Martha Inside-Seller, Minister of Home Economics: It started innocently enough, Mr. President. A few Chinese, wearing designer coolie hats, showed up to build the railroads. . . . Well, okay, they toiled like slaves in the broiling sun using only their bare hands to put steel rails across hot deserts and steep mountains, but that was the 1860s.

Then came the Chinese hand laundry places and Chinese restaurants. Soon, communities sprung up . . . you know . . . Chinatowns. Especially in San Francisco. It was so cute and charming. A couple of Chinese signs and strange sounding talk.

Hal Boring, Minister of Hot Air: Is anyone hot?

One of the participants fidgets and then runs his fingers through his thin hair several times. Patience is lost and he stands, demanding attention. The President gives him the go-ahead.

The Donald Duckman, Minister of Big Business: The Chinese are taking over all industry and my guys are scared. Next year, cheap Chinese cars will be imported, selling for only $1,995. The Chinese are formidable, unfair, and ruthless competitors. They undercut the market price by 80%.

And there are so many of them. They already control the manufacturing of toys, useless kitchen stuff, cheap plastic things, and trivial trinkets. And shoes! . . . Mr. President, it's an uncontrollable invasion of Chinese business snatchers.

The President nodded once and pointed at the man seated next to The Donald Duckman.

Fess-up No-Action Jackson, Minister of Sports: They have also infiltrated American sports. First it was Mah-jongg. Then ping-pong, figure skating, and gymnastics. Now they have a foothold in the NBA. What's that Chinaman's name, plays Center for the Lakers, Wan Tal Gyeye? What kinda basketball name is that?

Here's-My-52-Cents, Minister of Finance: Yo, Mr. Prez, me and my posse are worried sick because the Chinese pirate everything. They got a Chinese rapper named Ten-Cent. That gangsta copy my style and he's stealing fans with cheap, knock-off rap.

Professor Mensa, Minister of Intelligence: The Chinese are taking over our schools. They get all A's. Our kids can't compete.

Worst of all, the boys at intel report the Chinese now have the nuclear-tipped Long Dong strategic missile aimed at the West Coast.

One minister makes a show of wiping his brow with a handkerchief.

Hal Boring: It's hot in here. . . . Can't we open a window?

Dr. Ruth I-Really-Need-Some-Good-Sex, Minister of Demographics: Mr. President, China has 1.2 billion people—that's 600 million men. Every morning, America faces the strategic threat of 600 million Long Dong missiles firmly pointed right at our homeland. Not to mention all the little Wangs they are making.

Oh-How-I-Talk-A-Lot, Minister of Communications: They bought CNN and re-named it the Chinese News Network. All Chinese, all the time. I have no idea what they are talking about, but I think diversity is good. I enjoy the inscrutable faces.

The Donald Duckman: It's bad, Mr. President—they even control the fortune cookie market, and as a result, control our fortunes.

The President pressed his fingertips together and pursed his lips.

The President: So it really is a crisis crisis—I need solutions.

A warning buzzer sounded and DEFCON 4 changed to DEFCON 5. The advisors, who had been relatively subdued, became aggressive. Voices were raised and the polished table was pounded as each Minister insisted their policy ideas should be heard and action taken.

Fess-Up No-Action Jackson: My people are being mistreated. We can't let the Chinese take over baseball. It's time for social justice. I demand a Chinese boycott.

Dr. Ruth I-Really-Need-Some Good-Sex: I demand we give them free condoms to halt the epidemic and support their sexual revolution.

Martha Inside-Seller: The Chinese have traded Mao's Little Red Book for a Little Black Book. We should export ice cream so they gain weight and aren't interested in sex. I have my own brand of delicious cold treats that look great served in my brand of fine china and eaten with my brand of fine flatware—and each piece is hand-made by young artisans in a Chinese factory.

Dr. Ruth I-Really-Need-Some Good-Sex: Or, we tell them to pretend it's a popsicle, honey. . . . Of course, that would affect sales of your products, but it's a small sacrifice to make for the good of our country.

The Donald Duckman: I demand protective tariffs on anything made in China. It's the only way we can protect hard-working employees—it's the little guy who is getting hurt.

Oh-How-I-Talk-A-Lot: I demand more diversity, Mr. President. I want my Greenland TV!

A frustrated minister stood and pounded the table with his fist. His face appeared as if it had been badly sunburned during a 3-day desert walkabout.

Hal Boring: Did someone say green?

The standing, red-faced minister, who asked about green, was ignored. After an embarrassed silence, the minister returned to his seat.

Hulkster Hoganhero: Mr. President, the Chinese are invading like ants at a picnic. Everyone thinks Katrina was bad. Well, that's nothing compared to the flood of Chinese products coming into our ports. I demand we close the borders. Let me start passing out body slams.

Here's-My-52-Cents: Yo! I demand we boycott Chinese rappers and stop streaming Chinese music.

Martha Inside-Seller: I demand we wear plastic wristbands and put decals on our cars. We need to raise awareness.

Fess-up No-Action Jackson: I demand a million-man march. The Chinese are holding us down. Justice delayed is justice denied.

The red-faced minister, angry that nobody cared about heat, pushed his chair away from the table and raised his hands into the air. His face was flooded with perspiration *and* exasperation.

Hal Boring: I'm really getting hot and itchy. We've got to do something right now about the rising temperature in this room or we're all gonna die, real soon now.

Professor Mensa: I demand we spend more on education, for the children.

The President leaned back in his chair, rubbed his forehead with his fingertips, closed his eyes, and thought about the virtues of patience.

A high-ranking military man strutted into the room and walked to the podium, set to the right of the large screen that displayed the map of China. He rapped his knuckles for attention and all eyes turned to him.

Faded General Douglas MacArthur, Minister of Defense: I have returned, baby! I told Truman in '51 to nuke them Chinese back to the Ming Dynasty. Now look at what we face.
Mr. President, please look at the display with the flashing red dots in major American cities. Those flashing dots represent the Malwall stores in America.

The General turned to a military man seated at a computer workstation on the right side of the room.

Faded General Douglas MacArthur: Put it up on the board, Colonel.

The big screen display changed to show 64 squares of video feeds. Each feed was from a different American city and featured customers inside a large store filling shopping carts with consumer goods.

Hulkster Hoganhero: Mr. President, we've got live video from every Malwall store in America. We've been monitoring shoppers for years. Americans are buying everything and anything. They are like crack addicts—they can't get it fast enough.

The President: What do you propose I do?

Faded General Douglas MacArthur: I've got one million troops ready to rumble. My plan, while radical, will save America. There will be civilian casualties, but the loss of a few million Malwall shoppers will save the vast majority of citizens from the China Syndrome—

The red-faced minister, sweating profusely, jumped to his feet and interrupted the briefing, again.

Hal Boring: Look at me! I'm burning up—literally cooking! This hot foot crisis is more serious than any Chinese challenge we face. In fact, we've got to do something right now. If we don't take immediate action, I will spontaneously combust.

The faded old warrior shook his head and dismissed the warm weather alert raised by the red-faced minister.

Faded General Douglas MacArthur: Mr. President, my men are ready to roll through Malwall like crap through a goose. It's a failsafe plan we call Attention Malwall Shoppers. We send in the troops, seal off every store in America, and engage the Stealth bombers. Those little yellow smiley value faces will never know what hit 'em. We call it Shopper Shock and Awe—

The red-faced minister, with his hair smoking, moved next to where the old warrior stood. He slammed his open palm on the podium and demanded everyone in the room listen.

Hal Boring: I'm telling you it's really hot in here. The ice in my glass has completely melted. In just a few minutes, flames will be shooting out of my head.

Martha Inside-Seller: Hal Boring, you're wearing long johns, a wool suit and woolen cap, a parka, electric socks, and you're carrying a trendy cell phone and tablet—all made in China by Chinese who only work 14-hour shifts and live in fine factory housing. Those workers are just like the Chinese folks who lovingly crafted our railroad tracks 160 years ago. . . . And they gladly do this so we can have all the conveniences of the modern world . . . at a great price. So quit your bitching.

Here's-My-52-Cents: Yeah, chill homie.

The wise, old Chinese attendee, seated in wheelchair, waved his chopsticks to get attention.

Dr. Chopstick, Foreign Policy Advisor: This is Nixon's legacy, the Chinafication of the world. Like water running downhill, Chinese seek any path to world domination. We must defeat them.

The wheelchair minister paused and gave a harsh stare to those assembled around the table.

Dr. Chopstick: Our problem is not the illegal Mexicans. It's the parade of humanity from the People's Republic. We must start a crash program to finish the Great Wall and keep the Chinese inside.

Suddenly, while everyone watched, the wheelchair man radically transformed from a mild-mannered advisor into a man possessed with madness. As he transformed into his crazed self, he thrust the chopsticks like a knife, strained to get out of his wheelchair, and made Kung Fu moves with his one good leg and arm.

Dr. Chopstick: You Americans ran world for long time. Chinese tired of kowtow. We Chinese invent almost everything—firecracker, abacus, pigtail. China bring many good things, like bird flu, domination of Tibet, Fu Manchu facial hair, bamboo steamer, Chinese water torture, Chairman Mao, and people with the last name Chang.

Then, the wheelchair-bound madman caught himself and mellowed. He put down his chopsticks and reverted to his normal speaking voice.

Dr. Chopstick: Americans should stop doing business with the Chinese. Don't buy Chinese products. But it won't work. Americans only want things. All that television advertising.

The Ministers were stunned and the President heard a pin drop.

The wheelchair advisor waited, and with characteristic Chinese serenity, studied his audience. After a long pause, he spoke in whispered tones.

Dr. Chopstick: The Chinafication of the world may be a positive change for the good. Or it could be a terrible development. . . . It all depends on your perspective because, according to an ancient Chinese proverb . . . crowded elevator smell different to midget[1].

The President pondered and the Ministers sniffed the air. After a silence, all the Ministers spoke at once which escalated to an argument that featured name-calling, finger-pointing, and challenges to wrestle. The anger erupted into a free-for-all after

---

[1]Source: Internet, Website unknown.

Hulkster Hoganhero scored a body slam against Martha Inside-Seller.

The President pounded a gavel and called for order, but like the red-faced man, the President was ignored.

A fist fight erupted between Professor Mensa and Oh-How-I-Talk-A-Lot. There was assorted hair pulling, racial epithets, kicking of feet, and wagging of heads.

Hulkster Hoganhero put Donald Duckman into a sleeper hold.

And then, Hal Boring spontaneously combusted.

The Sit Room filled with Military Police who blew whistles, thumped heads, and took names. Eventually order was restored and the Ministers were escorted from the room, leaving the President alone.

The President, strained by the burden, pushed back his chair. He studied the threat board which showed the formerly blue U.S. turning red—the same color as China.

The President sighed and thought, *I can't tolerate this anymore. Nobody can run this country. Every one is a whiny, greedy special interest demanding their wants be fulfilled.*

The President pressed the intercom button and heard a woman's voice.

Betty Chang, Presidential Secretary and Confidant: Yes, Mr. President?

The President: Betty, maybe Dr. Chopstick is right. After all, 1.2 billion Chinese can't be wrong. I've made a decision. It's time to implement my China policy.

Betty Chang: Sir, what can I do for you?

The President: Please submit my resignation and get me on the next flight to Bali Hai.

Nurses

I arrived at Dachau on a cold, clear Bavarian morning in January 1994. Protected by my gloves, long johns, scarf, and American-made jacket. Safe, warm, and comfortable in my cocoon. Insulated from the outside environment—the penetrating cold—and distant from the monstrous reality.

I knew, and unjustly so, what a concentration camp was about. What the Holocaust was about. What death was about. I had seen the faded photos, watched the jerky black-and-white newsreels, and even read some of the horrific accounts.

But I did not understand. I did not experience. I was separated by time, generations, and events.

"Why do you go there?" my German mother-in-law asks.
I do not speak German and she does not speak English.
 My wife answers, "Because he wants to, Mama."
"Why does he want to go?"
"He just wants to go."

But is that all? Is this another tourist attraction to visit during my trip to Germany? Is this just some morbid curiosity? Why do I want to see this place?

My wife and I go to the nearby train station and study the map to identify the trains we will ride to Dachau—a place, on the map, like every other place. No special symbol. No special notes.

The train is filled with sad-looking men and women on their daily commute to work. Students, children, and a few elderly, too. For them, just another day in a long series. I look at the people and wonder what I will see this particular day. And I wonder about the real meaning of Mama's question, "Why does he want to go to a place of evil?"

The train slows and stops.

A male voice comes over the intercom, and with sharp German diction announces, "Dachau."

The place of the first German concentration camp. Where it began. Where the Nazis would learn. The doors open.

We walk along a road and ahead I see a high cement wall and a gate. Soon, the big iron gate, ominous and tall, is before us. "Cross my threshold," it commands. I take off my glove, reach out, and touch this gate.

It is real.

My hand is cold and I feel the layers of my protection peel away as I pass through the gate.

Inside, it is big, silent, and nearly empty. I see the guard towers and the killing zone between the razor wire fence and the high outside walls. The towers of control and the killing zone where hope died.

I feel weak and vulnerable and understand why I cannot escape. Why I am trapped. The design was perfected here. Keep them inside, or kill them. Two options. There was no way for a living being to flee. No way to freedom. Courage is all they had. Courage to live and face another day, in spite of the hell.

We view the museum exhibits, documenting the horrors of this place. The life-size photos of the living dead and of the bodies of those who passed. The exhibit of worn shoes, piled 4 feet high behind a glass enclosure 10x10. Only shoes remain. No one to wear them.

Life truncated.

There are pictures of medical experiment victims, taken in a focused, deliberate, sterile manner, documenting a victim's reaction to extreme physical experiments. They are cold pictures, as if snapped by an insurance adjuster documenting the destruction of inanimate objects.

But these were real human beings, tested like animals, looking at the camera, looking into my soul. Deep expressions of fear and pain. I am unable to help. They have tremendous courage to convey their fear and pain for eternity.

My face is cold.

We wander the camp. No guided tours. Only the crunch of our shoes on the gravel as we go from place to place, alone. There are few people here this winter day. We go inside buildings and read the signs. The kitchen and dining room for those who ran the camp. Administration offices—for those who made the decisions. The living quarters of the guards—those who enforced the rules.

Then, the prisoner areas—the outside grounds, the working areas, the barracks. I go inside the prisoner barracks and feel the confinement and despair of those condemned to sleep on the wooden racks. A place where courage slept.

There are no food and drinks in this sinister place. No visitor comforts at all. And none are wanted, nor deserved.

We wander, and then suddenly, jutting into the cold, blue sky, rising above everything, is a square, brick chimney. It is hidden from the rest of the camp, behind several rows of tall, barren trees.

It is a beacon, leading me to the center of evil—the building known as Barracks X.

Barracks X is a squat, single-story, long and narrow building. It is well-built, made of brick with square lines and German exactness. Not at all imposing; it resembles a small motel in America. A few windows and doors. It is late afternoon and colder. I feel the wind about my head and neck and re-wrap my scarf.

We approach and enter. We are alone, inside this building of death. We do not speak. We go from room to room and read the signs. Then we enter a windowless room with four ovens together and a fifth a short distance away. This is the place marked by the chimney. A place of efficiency. To burn bodies. Thousands of bodies.

The room is 20 x 30, with a low ceiling. Not at all large. The ovens have heavy, iron doors and are made of red brick and cement. They are long, narrow, dark tubes, just big enough for a body. There is a platform in front of each oven where the bodies are stacked and then pushed inside, head first. I stare deep into the ovens and try to fathom the horror. I touch the iron doors and the brick of the ovens. I move closer, put my face to the oven opening, and peer inside. Black. Black with soot. Black with death.

I study the room, this efficiently designed prototype for mass disposal. Brick walls, cement floor. Brick ovens. Austere, utilitarian. A simple room of fire, of incineration, of extermination. A room of death. I feel cold and pull my jacket tight.

I see a small brass plaque on a far wall. I move toward it, to read the message. I stand close. It is written in English. I read the inscription. I reach up and touch the plaque—a memorial to honor four British nurses executed in this room.

Nurses, who care for the sick and injured. . . . I am cold and numb. . . . Nurses, who heal and provide relief. . . . My heart is heavy and burdened. . . . Nurses, who hold and comfort. . . . I am alone and shivering.

Author's Note

I wrote this in March 2006, based on my 1994 visit to the Dachau Concentration Camp and Memorial Center. At the time, I was unable to verify the story of the four nurses honored by the memorial plaque. I wrote the story as I recalled the events of that day.

Later, I contacted the official Dachau Memorial Website to inquire about the plaque and the people honored.

The memorial plaque reads:

Here in Dachau on the 12ᵗʰ of September, 1944 four young Women Officers of the British Forces attached to Special Operations Executive were brutally murdered and their bodies cremated. They died as gallantly as they had served the Resistance in France during the common struggle for freedom from tyranny.

Mrs. YOLANDE E M BEEKMAN (née Unternahrer)
Croix der Guerre avec Etoile de Vermeil
Women's Auxilliary Air Force Seconded to Women's Transport Services (F.A.N.Y.)

Mrs. MADELEINE DAMERMENT
Légion d'Honneur Croix der Guerre avec Etoile Vermeil
Women's Transport Services (F.A.N.Y.)

Miss NOORUNISA INAYAT KHAN

George Cross Member of the Most Excellent Order of the
British Empire
Mentioned in Despatches Croix der Guerre avec Etoile de
Vermeil
Women's Auxilliary Air Force Seconded to Women's
Transport Services (F.A.N.Y.)

Mrs. ELAINE S PLEWMAN (née Brown-Bartroli)
Croix der Guerre avec Etoile de Vermeil
Women's Transport Services (F.A.N.Y.)

"But the souls of the righteous are in the Hand of God, and
there shall no torment touch them."

Further research revealed these women worked as nurses while
also working for British Intelligence behind enemy lines. They were
arrested by the German authorities and executed as espionage
agents.

There Ought To Be A Law

Let me propose a hypothetical: You are driving home after a hard day at work dealing with rules, laws, and assorted commands. In order to take the edge off the day, you consider visiting the new strip club in town.

Just as you pull into the parking lot to stop for a quick beer and ogle, your cell phone rings.

It's your wife.

Before you say hello you hear: "Would you pick up some Earth-friendly toilet tissue, vegan cracker spread, celery, and a gallon of organic ice cream."

It is not a question. It is a command.

Your automatic response: "Yes, dear."

Let us examine the specifics of the conundrum. After taking orders and commands all day, you believe it's Me Time so you turn into the parking lot.

Hey, the work day is over and now you can enjoy some simple, clean, harmless fun—after all, there are regulations governing the establishment.

Then the cell download begins. Your free will is hijacked and you are issued a new set of commands to follow. Your only options:

a) If you ignore your wife, and choose to go where you can fantasize about nookie, you will be served divorce papers. This means you will soon be following onerous demands issued by your estranged wife's Legalman[2].

b) If you choose to go to the whole foods market you have given up your desire to help a young lady pay her college tuition. You will also not get any real nookie upon your arrival at home. Well, that last sentence is biased and based on my personal experience, but that is beside the point.

The bottom line: You have no free will. None.

Commands, rules, and laws control human behavior and eliminate freedom. They are pervasive and are constantly issued by the authorities. They can be overt, such as: orders, threats, and demands. Or they can be disguised as: advice, suggestions, and cautions. They are presented in a multitude of ways. Such as:

Signs, tickets, and warning lights
Red ink correction marks
Admonitions from a dentist, plumber, or dry cleaner
Anything written in upper case
Just about everything written in lower case
Exclamation points
Talking points
Anything with a point, including a spear.

They consume enormous amounts of energy to create, obey, enforce, and punish. The situation has now become so onerous that

---

[2] Term coined by Robert J. Ringer, Winning Through Intimidation. p. 198. New York: Fawcett Crest, 1973.

once free men and women are slaves—held captive by a myriad of controls and restrictions. And these same people, who were once free and independent, now solely exist to obey the rules, follow the commands, and live by the letter of the law.

The erosion of our collective personal freedoms concerns me. So, in the interest of saving humankind and to fulfill a collegiate essay assignment, I will travel through time to examine why the first rule was created, what was the most ridiculous law ever written, and what will be the last command ordered. All in the space of fifteen hundred words—a rule issued by the teaching authorities.

One afternoon, with the expert help of a wild-haired Professor, I built a time travel machine out of my 1992 Buick Skylark. I would have preferred a time-traveling Delorean, but my student budget did not permit such an expensive undertaking.

I grabbed my cigarettes, jumped into the Buick, and pressed speed dial on my cell phone.

"Wild-haired Professor, can you hear me now?" I asked.

"Yes J M. Where do you want to go?"

"Take me back to the first rule ever created."

"Okay, just hit the gas—but be careful J M because I haven't got your cloaking power operational."

"No problem, Professor. I won't stay in any one place long enough to experience the rules of the time."

I took hold of the steering wheel and stomped on the accelerator. A flash of bright lights passed the windshield, my vision blurred, and I was transported back in time—to the year 20,000 B.C.

When the dust settled, I found myself inside the Buick parked on a grassy hillside, at night. A few hundred feet away, up the hill, I saw a cave lit by the glow of fire light. I exited the Buick, crept within earshot, and hid behind a large boulder.

Four ugly guys, who wore fur loincloths, squatted next to the fire. They had long stringy hair, terrible body odor, and odd-looking faces. They picked at their bodies, moved around like chimps, and looked like cavemen—heck—they were cavemen.

I identified three of them as Cro-Magnons. The fourth dude was a Neanderthal. Upon further scrutiny, I determined these particular Cro-Magnons were the first of a subspecies identified as Cro-Magnon Smart-a-tus.

Due to my extensive high school education, where I majored in Cro-Magnon, I knew the Smart-a-tus subspecies had an IQ one point higher than any previous Cro-Magnon. The single point higher IQ gave Smart-a-tus an incredible advantage—they were the Einstein's in a cave full of cretins.

Also, because they were Smart-a-tus, they had names. According to the anthropologist weenies who study these things, Smart-a-tus had two letter names because the other letters had not yet been invented. The Neanderthal, being a Neanderthal, did not have a name.

These particular Cro-Magnons allowed the small-headed Neanderthal to live in their cave because he could fight other Cro-Magnons who showed up to steal their woman.

Luckily, I studied Cro-Magnon as a second language and can translate their fireside chat of grunts and sounds.

Cro-Magnon Al and Cro-Magnon Ed sat together on one side of the fire. Cro-Magnon Yo and the Neanderthal sat opposite.

"Um, fire good," Al said.

"Mm, fire good," Ed said.

Smoke blew into Yo's face. He coughed and his eyes watered. "Agh, fire bad," Yo said.

Neanderthal grunted.

After a while, Al crinkled his nose, raised his eyebrow, and looked at Ed.

"It smell bad. From you, Ed?"

"No, Al, not me."

Serendipity struck as I determined this was the first lie ever told.

There were assorted Cro-Magnon and Neanderthal grunts and movements.

After a while Al said, "Maybe we need to invent a rule."

"What is a rule?" Ed asked.

"Something that controls cavemen from doing certain things."

"You mean like when Cro-Magnon Lulu gets mad and says no nookie? Is that sort of a rule?"

"It might be, but I think that is just Lulu's way."

"Oh."

There was a long pause. Finally Ed said, "Did you ever notice that Cro-Magnon Lulu is ugly—she has a misshapen head."

"Yes," Al said. He looked into the cave at Lulu, shook his head side-to-side, and said, "Why do other Cro-Magnons want to steal her? I don't get it."

There were more caveman grunts and movement.

"Why do we need to invent a rule?" Ed asked.

"I'm not sure, but I think we need one," Al said.

The Cro-Magnons sat and did nothing while Neanderthal chewed on a giraffe thigh bone. Cro-Magnon Yo grabbed some chestnuts roasting on the open fire and nearly burned his hand.

Neanderthal saw Yo take the chestnuts so he swung his giraffe bone and hit Yo upside the head. Yo fell backward and was knocked unconscious.

Neanderthal was amazed by the result of his strike. Al and Ed were shocked.

"Hey, Yo! Wake up!" Al said.

Neanderthal held the bone high, gave it a good eyeballing, and tilted his head sideways. He gripped the base with two hands and swung it down into the fire causing sparks and embers to fly.

Neanderthal smiled and turned to his right. He raised his club, and with great strength, hit a pile of bones causing pieces to fly into the air.

Neanderthal hit the old bone fragments again. Then he jumped up-and-down and enthusiastically beat the pile of bones over-and-over while screaming and jumping wildly—a Neanderthal run amok.

"He is out-of-control," Ed said. "What are we going to do?"

"I told you," Al said. "We need a rule."

Ed and Al looked at Yo, who was sprawled out and just returning to consciousness.

"I've got it," Al said. "The first rule."

"What?" Ed asked.

"The dude with the club gets to eat first."

Ed nodded in agreement.

And so that is how it all began.

After Yo sat up Al said, "I just made a second rule, Ed."

"What's that?"

"The guy with the club gets the first choice of the blondes and brunettes."

Ed nodded in agreement.

And so the rule-making continued.

Yo rubbed his head and looked at Neanderthal who wildly hit everything in sight with his club.

"You cretin," Yo mumbled, "why in the hell did you hit me?"

Neanderthal stopped, looked at Yo, and said, "I was following the rules. You touched my nuts."

I edged into the open so I could document the scene with a photograph, taken by my cell. Neanderthal spotted me and screamed hysterically. I figured he was getting pretty good with his club so I concluded my scientific observations—just-in-time to get a running start on my journey through time.

By now, all four cavemen were chasing me, under the mistaken belief I was plotting to take Lulu. I moved as fast as possible—extremely glad I had the foresight to wear my Air Jordans.

Unfortunately for me, Neanderthal and his club were closing fast. Evidently, in spite of a small head, Neanderthal was a world-record holder in the sprint.

I reached the Buick, jumped inside, and pressed speed dial.

"Professor, fire this muthha up before I become the first victim of assault with a deadly weapon," I screamed.

"Where to?"

"Onward to the most ridiculous law ever written."

"But there are two, J M—tied for most ridiculous."

"Send me to both!"

"Okay!"

I hit the gas just as Neanderthal jumped on the hood of the Buick. I saw him swing his club down to the windshield and a moment later I was parked behind a large basilica.

I slipped out of the car and read a text from the Professor that cloak power would make me invisible for short periods of time. I requested full cloak and a second later I was invisible. I hopped over a low fence, crept though a small cemetery, and stepped inside the basilica.

A guy wearing a white, pointy cap was seated at a long table which stood on a raised platform. I recognized him as a Pope from a long time ago. Several ugly clergymen, wearing monk robes, were seated either side of him.

An emaciated man, dressed in rags and with his hands and feet bound, stood before the men seated at the table. The prisoner was held upright by two Enforcers who had swords dangling from their belts.

"That's blasphemy," the Pope said loudly. "The Earth is round and revolves around the sun?" He elbowed Ugly Clergyman No. 1, seated to his right, in the ribs. "That is really stupid and that is *not* God's Law."

"Everyone knows the Earth is flat! That is God's law," Ugly Clergyman No. 1 said as he rubbed the spot where the Pope's elbow jabbed his ribs. "We are the center of the Universe."

The prisoner pleaded, "Forgive me, Your Holiness. I observed the horizon line appears to be curved. I am not insulting God. It is just an observation. You can see it too, Your Holiness."

"This is ridiculous," the Pope said. "The Earth is flat. That is God's Law."

"He speaks the devil's talk," Ugly Clergyman No. 2 said. "I say off with his head."

"I agree," Ugly Clergyman No. 3 said. "But first, let me take him to my chambers and counsel the poor soul. I will help him make peace with God before he is dispatched." Then Ugly Clergyman No. 3 smiled and added, "I like the way he looks in those rags. Maybe I can get a little nookie."

"No!" the Pope shouted. "There will be no horseplay with the unbeliever and homosexuals are *not* permitted by this God." The Pope pointed a stiff finger at Ugly Clergyman No. 3 and then at the prisoner. Then he ordered, "Off with both their heads."

My phone vibrated. At the risk of revealing my presence, I removed it from my pocket and saw a text from the Professor: *No cloak ten seconds. Get to Buick.*

Unfortunately for me, the Professor's ten second warning was actually only one second in real time. I materialized and so did the glow of my phone.

The Pope spotted me lurking in the back row of the pews and shouted, "The Devil dares enter the sacred place of worship. Bring him to me."

The Enforcers dropped the prisoner and ran toward me, swords drawn.

I spun around and pushed open the heavy door, intent on a speedy run to the safety of the Buick. I hurdled three headstones in the cemetery, cleared the low wall as if I was an Olympian, and dove headfirst into the open window on the driver's side of the Buick.

Unfortunately for me, the Enforcers were faster Olympians and each of them grabbed my shoes as I went horizontal. They pulled on my legs and partially removed me from the car. Just as I thought I would be next in line to greet the Pope, I rolled to the left and shoved the accelerator to the floor with my hand.

My Air Jordans were left behind, in the hands of the astonished Enforcers. But lucky for me, I saw the bright lights whizz past, and suddenly I was parked behind another low wall near a mosque.

I looked at my hand and realized I was invisible. I exited the Buick, jumped the low wall, crossed a small cemetery, and entered the mosque.

A guy wearing a green, pointy cap was seated at a large table which stood on a raised platform. I recognized him as a Grand Ayatollah from long ago. Several ugly imams, wearing robes, were seated either side of him.

A bearded, emaciated man, dressed in rags and with his hands and feet bound, was prostrate on a prayer rug. Two Enforcers, with scimitars dangling from their belts, stood either side of the prisoner.

"Infidel! You drew a representation of the Prophet Muhammad," the Grand Ayatollah said. "That is forbidden!" The Grand Ayatollah grabbed and jerked the beard of Ugly Imam No. 1, who was seated to his left. "There are to be no representations of Muhammad. That is the law!"

"Everyone knows God makes the rules," Ugly Imam No. 1 said. Tears of pain filled his eyes and he rubbed his chin where the Grand Ayatollah pulled on his beard. "The infidel must be punished. I say a beard for a beard."

The prisoner pleaded, "I beg you, Your Holiness. I had a dream Allah told me to draw him. I think I have drawn him well. He looks good. Let me show you."

"He had a dream? Allah told him?" Ugly Imam No. 2 said. "He is sacrilegious! I say off with his head!"

"Mercy please, Your Holiness. I meant no harm," the prisoner cried. "Allah told me to show the people a picture of Prophet Muhammad—it's just a simple drawing. And the Christians have all those pictures of Jesus."

The Grand Ayatollah raised his hand and said, "Do you think I am stupid? You are an infidel. There are to be no representations of the Prophet. That is the will of Allah. Off with his head!"

"Yes, off with his head," Ugly Imam No. 2 said. "But first, let me take him to my chambers and counsel the poor soul. I will help him make peace with Allah before he is dispatched." Then Ugly Imam No. 2 smiled and added, "I like the way he looks in those rags—I'm getting wood—maybe I can get a little nookie before he goes."

The Grand Ayatollah reached out and tore away a chunk of Ugly Imam No. 2's beard. Then he yelled, "Homosexual! There is *no* diversity in the Qur'an! That is the law of God! Off with both their heads!"

My cell vibrated so I hid behind a nearby wall. I pulled out my phone and hit speed dial.

The Professor answered, "J M, we are now close to the fifteen-hundred word limit for this story. There may be only enough free words remaining for you to travel forward in time—or return to the now and be present for your next collegiate lecture."

"I do not have all the facts," I said as I realized my invisibility cloak no longer functioned. "I must go forward in time and find out what is the last command ordered by humanity."

"J M, if I send you to the future, there may not be enough word space to bring you back to the now. You'll be stuck there for infinity because of the word-limit rule."

A mosque guard came around the wall and my cover was blown. The burly guard raised his scimitar and ran toward me.

Just as the guard brought his scimitar within cutting distance of my neck, I went invisible and dove to the floor. I rolled away from certain death, got to my feet, and ran to the Buick. I jumped inside and hit speed dial. Again!

"Professor, for myself and all humanity," I said. "Onward—to the last command ever ordered!"

"Back to the Future!" the Professor yelled.

I hit the accelerator and found myself parked near a building that resembled The Acropolis. I got out of the Buick and ran up the stairs to the entrance.

Inside, the huge structure had a polished white marble floor, marble colonnade, and a high ceiling.

Black slabs, which resembled tall headstones in a cemetery, surrounded me in every direction. Each slab was six feet high, three feet wide, and two inches thick and they stood three feet apart.

Nearby, I saw a low table and a burning incense stick. The unusual smell of the incense was familiar, but I could not place it. A tiny brass bell and a small handwritten sign were on the table. I approached and looked at the sign. It read: *Please ring for service.*

I picked up the bell and gently shook it. It made a pleasant sound which echoed throughout the huge room. There was a puff of smoke and a Magic Swami mysteriously appeared, hovering in midair seated in a cross-legged yoga position.

The Swami was bald and wore a purple robe. He smiled and waved his hand for me to sit down at the opposite side of the table.

As I sat, I was sure I had previously met this particular Magic Swami and then—I recognized him.

This Magic Swami was the same Magic Swami I met in 2006 at an Indian Restaurant in Fort Myers where I came seeking answers about the value of deception. Swami still had the same calm, confident, and clean shaven appearance, and the dude still looked ageless.

"Long time no see, Magic One," I said.

"Yes, Grasshopper. I know you have traveled far and long through time. How was your trip?"

"Pretty smooth Magic One, except about 2045 A.D. That's when I ran into a bunch of 90-year-old baby boomers driving aimlessly and slowly. How's life been treating you?"

"I reached Nirvana a long time ago, after we first met in Fort Myers." The Magic One smiled and added, "I am content and complete."

"What year is it now?" I asked. "And where am I, Swami?"

"It is the year 2066, my son, and you are in The Great Hall. This is the place where every single rule, law, or command created by humankind is recorded. Including the last one." Magic Swami paused, looked at the floor, and shook his head. "You, my son, are the final representative of humanity—there is no one left."

"I am the Omega man? What happened?"

Swami grimaced. "We had to pull the plug on humankind. Things got out of control."

"Really—you unplugged humankind?"

Swami bit the inside of his lip and closed his eyes. "Yes, Grasshopper, we had to take drastic steps." He looked me straight in the eye. "Even though humankind accomplished great achievements and made wonderful discoveries—humankind also had a dark, devious, uncontrollable urge—they created too many rules, laws, and commands."

"Magic One, tell me the story."

"In the beginning, it was good," he said. "We informed humanity: *Those who do not learn from the past are condemned to repeat it.* We thought this was good."

"Well, that's great advice and the reason I never re-married."

Swami nodded and said, "Humanity listened to our advice and wrote things down so society might avoid making the same mistake. However, many people ignored what others had already learned the hard way. They violated the rules."

"Why is that, Swam?"

"Because we gave humankind freewill." The Swami frowned. "That was a mistake—letting the individual think for himself—because freewill made humans selfish. First they wanted sex, then money. And then they were willing to deceive to obtain them.

"Because of the human urge for sex, people learned to lie. Rules and laws evolved to control the lying. Then commands evolved. All were used to control behavior, beliefs, and thoughts. The authorities kept passing laws. They could not stop."

I nodded because I understood about sex, money, and lying.

The Great Hall was quiet. Swami floated peacefully and I needed a cigarette.

"Magic One, why didn't humanity just ignore the rules when they became overbearing?"

"Because there was no place to hide." Swami became upset and clenched his fists. "The authorities placed rules, laws, and commands everywhere telling every single person what to do. Annoying. Restricting. Dictatorial."

"So Magic One, what led to you to pull the plug?"

"There were several reasons—authority figures continuously overstepped their bounds—too many injustices were carried out in the name of the law—and eventually the world became the ultimate nanny state which overran the individual freewill we granted humanity."

"Why did it start, Swami?"

"Because of sexual relationships between a man and a woman." The Magic Swami sighed. "It stems from the desire to have and control the other . . . and meanness."

"Wasn't gold the issue?"

"No, gold came later and was a by-product of the sex drive."

I pondered the issue while Swami enjoyed a zen moment. Eventually a question came to my mind.

"Magic One, what causes the urge to control others?"

"Emotions, my son. Fear, hate, jealousy, anger, envy, and greed. Humans want to control the emotions and behaviors of other humans."

"Why the meanness, Swami?"

"It was the philosopher Nietzsche who said it best: *Let man fear woman when she hates: for at the bottom of his soul man is merely angry; woman, however, is downright mean.*"[3]

"Yeah, Swami. I know a few mean women. Drove me to drink."

Magic Swami continued, "Angry men tried to control women with rules and commands. Women had free will. They resented the control and began to hate. They created their own rules for men and this escalated throughout all society.

"Eventually, people demanded more and more and it became fashionable to be overtly worried about the latest cause célèbre. Many people became angry and hysterical when their demands were

[3] Nietzsche, Friedrich. New Translation from German by Thomas Wayne. Thus Spake Zarathustra - A Book For All And None. New York: Algora, 2003. p. 50.

not met. This led to more demands which led to more rules, laws, and commands.

"The situation spun out-of-control because people complained *there ought to be a law* about everything that they found offensive, harmful, or discomforting—no matter how ridiculous.

"The lawmakers wanted more power so they extended the ability of lawmakers to 'make the world right.' This gave them more power to pass more laws so they had more control."

I sat quietly and thought about how free and independent people had been overrun by assorted laws, rules, and commands.

Finally I said, "Yeah, Magic Swami, I know. Mattress tags, do not eat yellow snow signs, coffee is hot cautions, fast food calorie warning labels, no Sunday alcohol sales, and instructions to apply deodorant only to the underarms. It seemed as if everything involving the future of humanity always required urgent, drastic action and a myriad of new rules. It got so bad that I could hardly sleep."

"My son, no one was happy. There was no fun." Tears filled Swami's eyes. "We had never seen anything like it. Finally came the trial lawyers. They sued us. They claimed humans had a class-action personal injury case against God. After we were served a summons demanding we appear in court, we decided that we'd had enough."

"Wow. That was the final straw? The trial lawyers?"

Magic Swami turned and pointed at the black slabs that stood behind him and said, "See these? . . . They are the entire collection of laws, rules, and commands."

"There sure are a lot of them."

"Yes. Too many," he said. "We tried to advise humanity to stop But they did not listen. . . . We sent George Orwell, who wrote how it leads to Big Brother—so people might understand they should be responsible for themselves and not let others decide what is best.

But humanity paid no heed.

"Then we sent Arthur C. Clarke. He presented these black slabs which listed every rule, law, and command ever written. Humanity did not listen to him.

"Large segments of the population viewed rules, laws, and commands like numbers, continuing on ad infinitum—and the more the better."

I turned around, looked at the black slabs, and asked, "The slabs contain the entire record of every rule, law, and command ever created by humankind?"

"Yes, my son. The Great Hall contains even the last one."

I pulled out a cigarette and started to light it. "That is a lot to comprehend Magic One. Mind if I smoke?"

Swami waved his hand and said, "You know the rules—no smoking inside The Great Hall." Swami then pressed a forefinger to his chin, looked to his left, and said, "It's time for me to leave."

"Wait, Magic Swami, one last question—"

There was a poof, a wisp of smoke, and the Magic Swami was gone.

I stood and looked about The Great Hall. In front of me were rows and rows of black slabs, stretching as far as I could see. I approached the nearest slab and observed my reflection on the highly polished surface. There were no visible marks—just a smooth, hard, shiny surface.

I touched the slab. It was cold, but as I ran my fingers over it writings magically appeared—listing the Ten Commandments.

I ran my fingers over a different slab and revealed the Bill of Rights. The next slab listed the Laws of the Jungle. And the next listed rules of etiquette, good manners, and courtesy. Then a slab that listed the Boy Scout Code of Conduct.

I touched many slabs and found the rules for baseball, archery, and every other sport and game, including Monopoly. There was a large section of slabs containing sign messages listing prohibited activities such as: No Standing, No Sitting, and No Sleeping. Another section of slabs featured very tiny print—the tax code.

There were slabs in every language and every form of writing. Some I could read and some I could not.

I wandered for hours examining the slabs which marked the final resting place for every law, rule, and command. I finally had enough and thought to venture outside The Great Hall for a smoke.

But even though I had explored the slabs for hours, I had not discovered the end rule, the last law, the final command. And where was the exit?

I worked my way back to where I met Swami. He was gone, but on the table, next to the bell and the burning incense stick, was a gold key.

I took the key, looked around, and noticed a door where one had not been before. Above the door was a green exit sign.

I made my way to the door and tried the handle. It was locked. I cautiously inserted the gold key and unlocked the lock. As I turned the doorknob, I looked at the wall on the right. There was a switch and a small hand-lettered sign. I bent close to read it. There it was—the end rule—the last law—the final command:

If you are the last to leave, turn off the lights.

Huck Meets A Pantsuit

"There was things he stretched, but mainly he told the truth."

— *Huck Finn*

In a rundown section of Sarasota, on a side street near a river, sits an old brick building that contains a mediator's office. The office has a windowless conference room sparsely furnished with a table and eight banged-up swivel chairs.

It is the place where Huck Finn, and his woman, Becky Thatcher, ended up after they retired to Florida and got bored. It is also a room full of stretchers.

On the conference table is a tray that holds numerous snack packages of potato chips. The room also has a short refrigerator filled with various soft drinks and bottled water. There are no decorations on the walls and a withered houseplant sits forlornly on top of the refrigerator.

On one side of the table, standing, is: Legal Pantsuit, a New York attorney; Account Pantsuit, a New York CPA; and Becky Thatcher, the Plaintiff. Each is smartly dressed in a freshly-pressed black pantsuit and each carries a leather briefcase with gold latches.

On the opposite side of the table is: Legalman[4], a former rugby player and English soccer hooligan; Numbers Runner, a hard-of-hearing bookie; and the Defendant, an aged Huck Finn.

At the head of the table is the Mediator. He is an old guy with white hair and a drooping moustache. He is dressed in a 3-piece white suit, and a shiny, chrome whistle hangs from a string around his neck.

The atmosphere is hostile and tense and direct eye contact is avoided. Numbers Runner is wearing ear buds and listens to an iPod. Huck wonders why there are no pictures in the room.

There are brief introductions and handshakes, and everyone takes a seat. The room is quiet, except for the squeak of the battered swivel chairs, which is rather annoying.

The Mediator gave a short, hard blow to the whistle and called the meeting to order.

"We are here to settle your divorce," he said. "We are going to work together and find a resolution that will make both of you happy." He gave a referee stare at Becky and Huck and added, "I have three ironclad rules that must be obeyed."

Huck felt an itch on his left ankle and wished it away.

After a moment the Mediator said, "Rule No. 1: Did you bring money to pay for this session?"

Becky and Huck nodded in agreement.

"Good," the Mediator said. "No. 2: No one is to leave this room until we have an agreement. There will be no breaks whatsoever. Agreed?"

Everyone nodded and Huck tugged at his tie.

"Excellent. We are making great progress as a result of working together," the Mediator said. "Now No. 3: There will be civility at

---

[4] Term coined by Robert J. Ringer, Winning Through Intimidation. p. 198. New York: Fawcett Crest, 1973.

all times—no swearing, talking out of turn, or stretchers. Please help yourself to the chips and drinks. Remember, civility! We are working together for the same reason—money."

Huck stood, went to the refrigerator, and used the opportunity to display civility.

"Becky, would you like a pop?" he asked.

"Defendant," Becky replied with a voice Huck barely recognized, "you know I only drink bottled water. Please give me one."

Huck placed a bottled water on the table for her, grabbed a soft drink, and returned to his swivel chair. As he sat down, he looked at the opposition. The trio of ornery female faces caused Huck's original itch to re-acquaint itself with Huck's ankle. Huck suspected the pantsuits, and his socks, might be the twin causes of his discomfort.

He reached below the table and scratched at his ankle. Then he pulled the sock down so he had direct access to his skin. By the time his fingernails reached that itch, a twin itch arrived, on the other ankle. It, too, demanded attention.

So Huck gave the second rogue itch some fingernail time. He also vowed never, ever, to be talked into wearing socks again. Or a suit.

After gaining a bit of temporary relief, Huck did his best to ignore the flare-up of double trouble, fearful the removal of his shoes and socks would create a bigger problem.

The Mediator gave a nod and asked the Plaintiff's side to begin.

"Mrs. Thatcher," Legal Pantsuit said, "has a fair and reasonable settlement to propose." She smiled at Huck and continued, "In recognition of Mrs. Thatcher's desire to own the marital home, and the defendant's desire to keep the marital residence, we offer the trees on the property to Mr. Finn." She glanced at the Plantiff and added, "Of course, my client would be the sole owner of the house.

This offer is extremely generous and non-negotiable."

Account Pantsuit chimed in, "Ms. Thatcher is making a *very* reasonable offer." She glanced at a paper she held and looked at the Mediator. "I have examined all the numbers and determined this offer is more than fair to Mr. Finn. This is a sincere effort to settle this silly litigation. . . . The Defendant will get 84 trees and my client gets none."

Huck's Legalman looked over the top of his eyeglasses at Account Pantsuit.

"Mr. Finn," Legalman said, "has been the only one to care for the trees and landscaping during the marriage. He is entitled—"

"It's my turn to talk," an irritated Account Pantsuit replied. "Don't interrupt me with lies about the work Mr. Finn claims to have done during the course of the marriage."

The Mediator held up his hand and turned to Legalman.

"Please remain silent," the Mediator said. "After the Plaintiff's side has finished their presentation, I'll give you plenty of opportunity to respond."

The Mediator's request to remain silent caused a third itch to arrive on Huck's right forearm, joining the party started by the ankle itches.

Legal Pantsuit adjusted her jacket and smiled at the Mediator.

"It's in Mr. Finn's best interest," she said, "to accept our generous offer and settle today. That way he can enjoy trimming his trees in the Florida sunshine and get back to floating down the river instead of wearing a cheap suit, moldy wing tips, and wasting time in an attorney's office."

Itches, like raindrops, never arrive solo. Sure enough, another itch soon fell from the sky and attached itself to Huck's hind end.

Huck remained silent and attempted to appear civilized.

Legal Pantsuit stared at Huck as if she was preparing to stab him with a rusty switchblade.

"Of course," she said, "we expect Mr. Finn will do his landscaping work at midday—but only on Monday, Wednesday, and Friday."

The pantsuit team nodded in agreement.

The Mediator's chair squeaked as he turned toward Huck and his crack legal team.

"What do you guys think of this as a starting point?" he said.

Huck immediately surmised he was winning and that rumors of his demise were certainly exaggerated.

"I think Ms. Thatcher could do better," Legalman said. "After all, according to the fine print she gets the martial home, stardom in the book business, a retirement fund, the savings accounts, and the hand-built raft."

Because all itches felt ignored, a fifth itch was encouraged to claim territory on Huck's back, right between his shoulder blades. A civilized Huck suppressed the urge to scratch any member of the itch conga line.

"As I understand the proposal," Legalman continued, "my client gets the marital trees. This invites two questions: Does my client leave his trees at the property and where is he going to live?"

"Mr. Finn can leave the trees on the property," Legal Pantsuit answered, "as long as he cleans up after them." She looked at Becky. "I'm sure my client would not object if Mr. Finn built himself a tree house residence—a temporary structure, of course."

"Only for one month!" Becky cried. "And he cannot use the bathroom inside the house. Even if he has to go No. 2!"

Huck dropped all pretenses of being civilized and made quick movements to remove his shoes and socks so as to satisfy the ankle annoyers. Relief was achieved, and Huck's feet felt better too, able to breathe fresh air.

Account Pantsuit tilted her chin upwards and sniffed.

"Mr. Finn," Legalman said, "is entitled to his separate property he had before the marriage and half of the marital assets. Your settlement offer does not take that into account. And what about the raft—that was his pre-marital property!"

Huck fidgeted, loosened his tie, and pulled at his shirt to untuck it.

Becky took the last sip of the bottled water and set the empty on the table with authority.

"He never," she said, "worked a day during our marriage."

Now that one was a real stretcher, so it was time for Huck to step into the ring with the pantsuits, even if he was barefoot.

"We starred in a classic book," Huck said as he stood. "It didn't happen in a vacuum—yer famous and respectable because of me and Tom and Sam. You got magical expectations and you ain't even proposed anything reasonable."

"Sit down, Mr. Finn," Legal Pantsuit commanded, "haven't you learned proper English yet? And don't talk with ain't." She scratched an itch on her nose. "Think hard Mr. Finn, even if it's difficult for you, because she is giving you all the wood from the trees. Build a house. Or better yet, build a raft and float out of her life. My client is under no obligation to do the work for you. She will not do for you what you can do for yourself."

"What . . . build me a tree house?" Huck said. "I don't even git me a hammer from our joint tool collection?"

Becky gave Huck the stink eye.

"I should have never left Tom for you," she said. "You're lazier than him. It was the biggest mistake of my life."

"Yeah, well Sawyer can have you back," Huck replied. "Maybe he can learn you to whitewash a fence."

Account Pantsuit sniffed the air again and made a face of disdain.

"I smell foot odor," she said while glaring at Huck. "Who didn't wash their feet today?"

Becky stood, pointed at Huck, and yelled, "It's him. He never washes his feet. I had to live with that barnyard smell all those years! He's scum!"

"Scrum?" Legalman said.

"Let's calm down," the Mediator said. "Remember civility and behave yourselves. Don't make me blow this whistle."

Huck raised his hands above his head.

"I ain't gonna be homeless," he said. "Yer suggestin' I live in a tree? That's not what I've grown accustomed to—you knowed I liked bare feet when we got married cuz I didn't wear shoes to the ceremony."

Legal Pantsuit curled her thin lips.

"Your feet stink!" she said. "You have to get out of the house Mr. Finn! Go find a place to live." She smoothed her lapels and added, "Mr. Finn, you can have all of the leftover funds in the piggy bank if you agree to leave today."

Her offer didn't sit well with Huck's collection of itches, so they all made a jump together and alighted on the back of Huck's neck.

Huck, pleased that all of the malcontents arrived in the same place, at the same time, scratched strongly for relief.

Released from his itch torment, and to throw the pantsuits off their game, Huck grabbed a bag of Multigrain Sun Chips from the tray on the table. He tore them open and munched on the crunchy, whole grain food.

"Mmm, these are good," he said. "Anyone want a pop?"

Thatcher glared at Finn.

"You know I don't drink that stuff," she said. "It's bad for my health."

Legalman followed Huck's lead and moved into offensive position. He leaned across the table toward Legal Pantsuit.

"Mr. Finn worked for half the marital assets," he said. "If she gets to star in the books until the end of time, he should get the house. . . . It seems like your side wants all the chips."

"I really like these Sun Chips," Huck said. "Accordin' to the package, whole grains is delicious. Did you ever try 'em?"

"Mr. Finn," the Mediator said, "please don't talk with your mouth full."

"See? I told you so," Becky said. "He's scum!"

"I ain't scum," Huck said. "These chips are really good. Anybody up for take-out 'cuz I'm hungry."

The Mediator stood as if he was going to throw a penalty flag.

Instead he said, "Mr. Finn, you agreed to the rules. We will not leave this room until a settlement has been reached." He pointed a crooked finger at Huck. "By the way, Mr. Finn, you have a chewed chip stuck on your chin."

"He's the kind to eat everything and leave nothing for the others," Becky said. "I told you he was scum!"

"Scrum?" Legalman said. "Did someone say scrum . . . are we scrumming?"

Suddenly, all of the pantsuits grabbed at the remaining packages of snack chips, looking for Sun Chips.

Huck was at first surprised, then amazed, and finally delighted, to watch as all three pantsuits fought among themselves over the chips. There were lapel grabs, pointed-toe shoe kicks, and bitch slaps.

The Mediator put the whistle to his mouth, blew loudly, and waded into the fight.

Numbers Runner, who was asleep, woke up.

"Yeah, strumming," he said, "like Roberta Flack sang in *Killing Me Softly* . . . scrumming my pain with his song. I can dig it."

"I knew it!" Legalman yelled. "Scrum!" He jumped from his chair and hurled himself into the mass of pantsuits fighting over the last bag of Multigrain Sun Chips.

Legal Pantsuit grabbed her briefcase and slammed it against

Legalman's head. Lucky for Huck's team, their lawyer was not even fazed.

Numbers Runner jumped into the fray and was double-teamed with a finger shake and head wag administered by two pantsuits. Things escalated and soon Legalman and Legal Pantsuit were going at it tooth and nail.

When it was clear that Legal Pantsuit was losing, she brandished a swivel chair and yelled, "Tell it to the Judge! Your client is scum!"

"I love the smell of scrum in the morning!" shot back Huck's guy as he dodged finger jabs from Account Pantsuit while he simultaneously avoided Legal Pantsuit, who wielded a swivel chair weapon-of-mass-destruction.

Huck's lawyer was in his element. He loved hand-to-hand combat mediation and he stood tall and strong, fighting for what he believed as the room filled with flying swivel chairs and stretchers.

The Mediator waded into the fight and blew his whistle many times, but it had no effect on the combatants. Eventually, a hothead pantsuit grabbed the Mediator, lifted him over her head, and proposed a neck-breaker as chaos overtook the room.

After lots more fighting, Huck sensed the time for the session was coming to an end. So, in the confusion, he grabbed the last bag of Sun Chips and slipped out the door.

Huck shed his suit jacket, tie, and pressed shirt, and along with his shoes and socks, tossed them into an empty elevator shaft. Then he pulled a corncob pipe from his front pants pocket, stuffed the pipe with tobacco from a pouch, and lit it. He took the back stairs to the ground floor and let himself out of the building.

Meanwhile, the scrum and whistle blowing continued unabated, as Huck journeyed to meet his friend, Jim, at a nearby watering hole.

Why On Earth Did We Build It?

Elderly people need a warm place to live. That's because they are old and slow—they cannot inhabit a cold place because if they go outside they move too slow and freeze. Elderly also like golf which is impossible to play on a snow-covered course.

So, seeing a need, a few guys with hammers came to Fort Myers, Florida. The men with hammers, along with the help of day laborers, worked to nail two-by-fours together. The land was cheap, the weather was good, and the hammerheads made some dough when they sold the finished product—houses for retirees.

Good news travels fast and good news about money travels even faster. Soon other hammerheads heard about the gold rush. They were drinking Budweiser, in Erie, during a blizzard. After a couple of more beers, they decided they could also employ day laborers—while their frigid wives could warm to outdoor sex during the sunny days of January.

So they came.

You know what? Those new hammerheads sold all of their assembled two-by-fours. And they also discovered a man could fish during February dressed in shorts, a wife-beater T-shirt, and no shoes.

Then scientific rumors, linking sunshine to longevity, zoomed around the Internet and stopped in Wisconsin for a visit. Soon the elderly in Wausau, who were tired of life in a city with an un-spellable name, gave up ice fishing and drove to Fort Myers.

But there was a problem.

Fort Myers had only one supermarket. Now, a single supermarket serving Fort Myers had not been a problem for many years. However, one day the entire Fort Myers region became gridlocked because there were so many people in town at the same time.

The police traced the gridlock to a pair of elderly men who got out of their Lincoln Towncars and had a slow-motion fistfight over the last blue parking space near the front door of the only place to buy bran, hemorrhoid cream, and condiments.

The Fort Myers mayor, a good old boy named Grafton, decided more shopping areas would be a convenience to the community and would keep the old men from joining various parking lot gangs.

This also had the additional benefit of aiding Grafton's brother, Bubba, and indirectly, the Mayor himself. Because Mayor Grafton could whisper to Bubba, during church services, secret plans for new shopping centers.

Bubba, being a well-connected, friendly chap with a weight challenge, had a cousin who was a modest banker manager in Fort Myers. His name was Johnny Blu.

Bubba informed Johnny Blu he could pay off a gambling debt to the Gambino family if they both purchased the land before it was re-zoned.

This idea appealed to Johnny Blu because he needed to get rid of the casino debt-collection thugs who visited his office on a regular basis. Johnny Blu also wanted to relocate to Vegas and divorce his fat second-cousin whom he married while on a bender.

So, the soon-to-be shopping center land was secretly purchased, re-zoned, and developed, all in sixty days. Johnny Blu made it to Vegas and Bubba drove a brand new Hummer to his new ranch named Lehigh Acres. The citizens were pleased and Mayor Grafton won reelection with a 98% vote. Best of all, the elderly citizens in Fort Myers could use coupons at two supermarkets.

However, there was a fly in the ointment—more people arrived in Fort Myers and some were kung fu fighting over the last blue parking space at the new supermarket from the day it opened.

Meanwhile, a bunch of baby boomer proctologists in Detroit were being sued by trial lawyers. These same proctologists were also tired of listening to unruly old men who complained, "Everything hurts, Doc. And my bowel movements are irregular." Like most doctors, this group also wanted to play golf in February while dressed in polo shirts and loafers without socks.

A guy named Zhivago was one of these doctors. Doc Zhivago was an émigré from Russia and he did not like winter—he had experienced enough cold as the head proctologist at the gulag in Siberia. One day he told his doctoring buddies about the wonderful weather in Fort Myers and that only modest "lean-to-style houses" had been constructed.

Doc Zhivago, and few doctor friends, pooled their money and created a real estate investment company. They bought land in Fort Myers, hired an unknown but "famous" golf course designer, and built a private golf course surrounded by really nice second homes.

The proctologist real estate investors built a tall wall around their new castles to protect them from the marauding natives—and also to keep cheapskates from sneaking on to the golf course. It made sense to them because they were rich doctors and that is what kings did.

They also figured that placing a McMansion behind a tall wall was cheaper than recruiting a private army to guard the palace while they were in Detroit fixing people who did not have enough sense to get out of the cold.

A few designer fruitcakes saw the McMansions. They joined the gold rush and sold overpriced kitchens, furniture, and draperies to the new residents. Then luxury car manufacturers, exclusive hotels, and trendy boutiques wanted part of the action. Fort Myers even attracted two professional baseball teams who desired warm sunshine for Spring Training.

So a baseball stadium was built. Then another.

Soon the entire region was awash in day laborers, two-by-four sales reps, McMansion hustlers, and a few local people who put bumper stickers on their cars which read: *When I get old I'm going north to drive slow.*

All of this excitement, and people, led to out-of-control growth and the "I want more" mentality. Everyone was making money, or thought they would because, "There was no controlling legal authority."

The dollar bill drove everything and everyone tried to maximize their monetary gain by negotiation.

This is normal behavior. And rational.

Why, you ask?

Because if you visit Big Auto Sales, on the sage advice offered by a commercial announcer who yells about the fabulous electric cars for sale, you negotiate the price of your next automobile purchase.

Or you drive to another dealer whose commercial announcer yells you can buy a similar car for less.

Only a moron wants to pay more than necessary for a product. And only a moron would sell something for less than it is worth. After all, you must work for the money—and who wants to work more than necessary?

Or listen to the yelling about car deals.

Of course, it costs lots of money and takes lots of negotiation to build something nice and quaint. That's why all the cozy seaside towns in the Northeast have house prices starting at—put pinkie finger in mouth, shave your head, and say, "one billion dollars."

The huge migration to Fort Myers of people who wanted to retire in style and drive a Japanese luxury car caused real estate prices in Detroit to crash and GM auto sales to fall.

News about cheap real estate in Detroit spread to folks in the Middle East who were tired of sand traps, camels, and really hot weather.

Soon, Detroit became home to the largest group of Arab-Americans. The new residents stimulated the local economy with convenience stores and mosques. They also bought large cars so they could move their wives and children around the city. GM was happy and so were the leaders of Detroit who now had a group of pioneers willing to sacrifice and work hard.

In spite of all the un-managed growth in Southwest Florida, one community stood united and posted a Keep Out sign for fast food mascots and big box stores. The citizens of this community did not want strip malls, franchise restaurants, stop lights, nudie bars, or car lots in their neighborhood. They also did not like overnight parking, visitors who littered, and people who disliked turtles.

So they declared their own fiefdom: The Kingdom of the Protected Island.

The early Islanders had good ideas about controlled growth way back in the 1970s. They created a Mission Statement which made it okay to ban chain stores and hammerheads who wanted to construct skyscrapers.

The theory worked well for the people residing on the island, who also happened to be just like Bubba and Johnny Blu—that is, they owned the land.

Things in Kingdom were good for many years. The native beach bums communed peacefully with the mosquito population, lived modest lives, and no tall structures invaded the natural shoreline and beaches.

However, the controlled growth policy of the Kingdom had a severe unintended consequence: the tremendous inconvenience of a two-hour drive in late afternoon traffic to get to an off-island supermarket where a case of Old Milwaukee beer could be purchased for less dough.

Over time, because the Kingdom valued low density and trees, a piece of the Kingdom became expensive. Eventually, the early settlers were priced out of the real estate market. Reluctantly, they sold out or faded away.

New citizens bought real estate in the Kingdom because they liked the idea they were *not* able to buy a Happy Meal on the island.

Some of these new residents made lots of money shorting GM stock as day traders. Some of them made money flipping real estate. And the rest of the Kingdom's landowners were happy because the air was filled with rumors their home was worth millions.

One summer day a big wind blew off many roofs and downed nearly all the trees in the Kingdom. When the citizens were permitted to return to their homes, they stared in awe at the storm damage and wondered if they still lived in paradise.

Adding to the burden of storm clean-up, real estate taxes were increased to pay for the new schools, roads, and traffic lights in the region.

Then insurance companies joined the party and increased the rates for hurricane and flood insurance. The premium increases forced some of the Kingdom residents to eat cans of dog food to survive.

Finally, after years of wrangling and construction, a new, gigantic cement bridge rose from the waters of the bay, linking the Kingdom to the mainland.

The Kingdom was under siege and the citizens could not raise the old drawbridge to insulate themselves from free market forces at work in Fort Myers.

This was because the trial lawyers, and everyone else from the cold, came South following the gold rush. They all wanted a piece of the pie because it's the American Way.

Things got bad—Fort Myers had absolutely no room for more people and terrible Feng Shui. A painful question had to be answered: *Why on Earth did we build it?*

Everyone became hostile, frustrated, and pointed fingers. Only the old people with irregularity were happy by comparison.

The citizens cried out, "What do we do now?"

Then it happened—an answer from beyond.

Nine different men materialized in Fort Myers—one by one. They were ghostly, had odd haircuts, and wore old baseball uniforms. People stopped and stared at the mysterious apparitions. Someone said they were the 1919 Chicago White Sox baseball team.

Then an old baseball fan recognized one of the men. He exclaimed, "That's Shoeless Joe Jackson!"

Shoeless Joe smiled, walked to the old fan, and said, "We're here to get in on the action."

"You're here for Spring Training and America's Favorite Pastime?"

"No, not baseball," said Shoeless, "America's other favorite pastime—to make money."

Shoeless Joe then turned the nearest real estate agent, who amazingly, was standing nearby. Shoeless asked, "Got any good deals?"

The old fan shook his head and muttered, "Say it isn't so, Joe."

On Truth And Lies In A Global Sense[5]

Warning! The following is intended for well-adjusted people with a sense of humor. If you can be offended in any way, do not read. Put this down immediately and seek counseling. No Chinese/Indians were injured in the production of this story.

However, John Travolta and the former residents of Biosphere 2 want the GPS coordinates of my island estate so they can plan an air raid.

"Once upon a time, in some out of the way corner of that universe which is dispersed into numberless twinkling solar systems, there was a star upon which clever beasts invented knowing."

Friedrich Nietzsche, 1873.

One day, humankind invented buying. With all due respect to Mr. Nietzsche, the invention of buying was far more important than the invention of knowing. Knowing is just a disorganized stub on the evolutionary tree of humanity and was invented in 1978 by an esteemed human named John Travolta. Mr. Travolta also invented

---

[5] On Truth and Lies in a Nonmoral Sense. Nietzsche, Friedrich, 1873.

disco, the Church of Scientology, and the private ownership of large jets.

Actually, it was womankind who invented buying. Mankind invented hitting. Together they formed humankind and created the society we have today which features these two inventions in a myriad of styles and forms run amok. These inventions are even more reptilian and powerful than the urge for sex. That is to say, every evil on our floating blue orb, environmental or otherwise, can be traced back to the invention of buying and hitting.

Now knowing, or knowledge, such as disco or Scientology, travels around the planet faster than light speed. The coconut wireless, all gossip all the time, spreads misinformation and dissimulation to every part of the globe enthusiastically and instantaneously.

This explains why my ex's posting about my size on Facebook was fodder for "jokes" by a remote Borneo cannibal tribe. The lost headhunter cannibals had discovered my disturbing, personal misinformation also posted on Match.com.

Because the headhunters "knew" way too much about my personal shortcomings, they created a YouTube channel warning tribal women everywhere not to date a certain J. M. Fisher.

I made an attempt to correct the huge distortion by contacting the tribe via smoke signal and drum message. It is interesting to note that during my "old-school instant message session" I learned the lost headhunters wanted big screen televisions, vegetable juicers, and Ginzu knives. They also informed me they wanted cable TV so they could watch wrestling and QVC, but they made no mention of disco, Scientology, or Mr. Travolta and his jets.

They also asked a rather strange question: *Why does the NSA monitor our smoke signals and drum messages?*

I instant drummed this reply: *Because they are recording every form of human communication to find out if the truth has ever been told by anyone. Unfortunately, after they were caught lying about their secret project, they blamed the entire affair on a rogue nerd programmer who was angry about a social media post made by an ex-girlfriend.*

The remote Borneo cannibals followed-up with: *We've already read the news posted by your ex-girl. . . . Can you confirm the rumor that the NSA has a secret machine and will travel back in time to record every human communication ever muttered, including the ones between Adam and Eve?*

I instantly replied: *They informed me that they do not have a time travel machine, so I ask you, whom do you believe, the NSA or your lying eyes?*

This proves my point regarding knowing: Knowledge, in all forms and mis-forms, seeks the light of exposure—there are no lasting secrets *anywhere.*

Or, to write it another way: Ideas, facts, information, truths, dissimulations, mis-truths, lies, and rumors are disseminated like dandelion seeds in a hurricane wind—and they move around the planet and influence anyone who is alive. Even after the originator is dead and gone.

Thus, when a starving guy, wearing a white lungi[6] in India, or a bamboo hat in China, watches a Super Bowl commercial that shows a bikini clad buxom blonde serving an American couch potato a Budweiser, he thinks: *I want that.*

Plans for hitting and taking soon follow.

Furthermore, when the Chinese/Indian man tells his wife he is going to his place of employ—the local Nike factory—to grab some shoes and run to America to steal the bikini girl, his wife puts the kabash on a portion of the plan involving a theft.

"You don't need to steal the bikini girl," she tells him. Instead of

---

[6] Lungi—traditional men's clothing in India consisting of a short length of material worn around the thighs like a sarong. www.rbcradio.com/clothing.html 5/25/07.

taking bikini girl, the wife demands her man, dressed in his bamboo hat and white lungi, spend his money and bring back a gold necklace. And some Chanel #5. And an $800 Louis Vuitton handbag.

Then sensing his weakness, the man's beautiful, unmarried 19-year-old daughter, Sanya Li, jumps into the family fray and demands Hollister low-rise jeans, Britney Spears music, and a car.

Our hero makes a vague comment as to why.

In response, the young lady swells with tears and runs to her bedroom, which she shares with 16 other siblings, and yells, "You don't love me!"

Driven by the love a father has for his daughter, our hero relents on his American Dream and also makes promises to give his daughter money so she can see the new movie, *Pirates of the Caribbean.*

Unfortunately, even though our heroic Chinese/Indian man is the village leader, he has barely enough money to buy seeds so he can grow biofuel to power his generator so he can watch Super Bowl commercials with his village buddies.

Worldwide communication, education, and "knowledge," coupled with humankind's natural desire to succumb to promises of instant riches and material things, has motivated our hero, and his family, to improve their lot in life. Advertising and envy have caused them to believe they will only be happy if they own material things, and they are convinced they can consume their way to happiness.

So the consuming demon is released and soon the entire village becomes consumed with consuming. Or, to incorrectly paraphrase former Senator Earnest Hollings, "There's a lot consuming going on out there in China and India."

Now, you may believe the worldwide buying frenzy is limited to beer, running shoes, big screens, and designer names. However, you would be mistaken, my dear reader, because buying extends into everything.

For example, our hero decides that drinking Budweiser will make him more attractive to the village sweeties. So instead of traveling to America, he uses his cell phone and Fed Ex to order a case of Bud in time for the next Super Bowl.

The Budweiser company in St. Louis is in a worldwide competitive fight for market share with many other beverage producers, including Heineken and Corona. In response, the Bud company submits an urgent request to the U.S. Dept. of Commerce for a special alcohol export license and claim the sale to China/India will result in a positive effect on the U.S. balance of trade and thus an improved economy—and the swelling of America's IRA and Keogh accounts.

It's an election year, so the export license gets approved via an announcement by a Presidential contender wearing a baseball cap and standing on a beer vat in Missouri.

Later that month, an oceangoing superfreighter sits empty after unloading a cargo of made-in-China/India George Foreman grills, cheap-looking pool loungers, hand-painted holiday ornaments, and other fine products destined for the place of the blue light special and the yellow-smiley-faced-price-cutting-guy. And in the end, to be consumed by people like my ex.

The single case of Budweiser, ordered by our hero, is the only item loaded on the superfreighter which returns to the Port of Hong Kong/Bangalore.

Over the next two weeks, the case of Bud makes its way to the Chinese/Indian village where our hero resides, arriving many days after the product expiration date.

Our village leader, overjoyed at receiving his good fortune from America, consumes the entire case of Bud happiness in a single sitting—as he tries to reach the cool nirvana enjoyed by the people who appear in the Super Bowl commercial.

Unfortunately for our guy, his drinking leads to a massive headache and nausea. So he stumbles to the local health care facility in search of Western wonder knowledge about cures. The medical staff, who have been sort-of-trained in a Western country and are looking to be appointed Minister of Health, determine they have discovered the first outbreak of human contracted Avian Flu.

They immediately get on CNN Breaking News and demand worldwide support to counteract this insidious illness and prevent widespread death. They are convinced the Nobel Peace Prize people are watching and they will be recognized for the importance of this announcement for all humanity and be awarded a big cash payout. Just like the kind Ed McMahon gives away.

John Travolta happens to be watching CNN Airport News when the breaking story is aired a week later, for the 300th time. Mr. Travolta is at the airport on a layover while jetting himself around the world promoting his role as a transvestite, who dresses in a red tutu and high heels, in the important musical docudrama, *Hairspray.*

Mr. Travolta immediately decides that helping sick people in China/India is more important than selling tickets to his new movie. He determines he can fill his jets with stuff from his Hollywood friends and so he coordinates a Live JetAid music show, with the help of Bob Geldof, Willie Nelson, and Al Gore.

These four elderly guys secretly believe they have a strong resemblance to the lads from Liverpool whose imagination, music, and lyrics changed the world in the 1960s—and these four elderly guys believe they can do the same.

The tremendous outpouring of human compassion at Live JetAid is in direct contradiction to the beliefs of hatred stirred up by the Islamofascist terrorists, who want to live in the 8th century, keep their women under wraps, and fly jets into buildings—proving the world is still a dangerous place.

The problem is there was an overreaction and our hero only needed a single Bayer aspirin and lots of fresh drinking water. In any event, this proves everything is connected—something I have "known" ever since they cut my umbilical cord when I was two years old which caused me to pump my tiny fists in the air and buy my own sustenance.

Jumping back to our couch potato Super Bowl American, we learn he is an up-and-coming district salesman with the Anheuser-Busch company named Mike. One morning Mike is standing by the office water cooler and he learns about the sale of the case of Bud to our friend in China/India. This young gentleman, a graduate of the university business school and who attentively listened to lectures regarding the growing economies of Asia, puts two-and-two together and gets the idea that he can "do like Nixon."

So, in order to meet his company's mandated sales quota, which supports the elevated NYSE stock price, Mike makes plans to open the Chinese/Indian market to Budweiser consumption one drinker at a time. He figures this is a fool-proof way to rise above other hard working Bud sales reps, earn the big dollars, and thus actually get a bikini clad buxom blonde and end his loneliness.

A couple of hard-working weeks later, our intrepid beer salesman goes to the airport full of enthusiasm for his trip to the Asian subcontinent. Unfortunately, Mike waited in a long line at check-in, endured a TSA pat-down, and missed his plane.

This caused him a mental breakdown in the airport lounge because his boss fired him while yelling, "You let those foreign beer competitors from Holland and Mexico take our market share!"

But luckily for our broken beer salesman, an airport visitor named John Travolta walked by and offered Mike a jump seat on his private jet which was ready to leave for China/India.

So after a rough start and 24 hours of flying, Mike arrived

disoriented in the Orient. He checked his Blackberry and confirmed all of his preset business appointments and realized he needed a good night's rest. He looked around for a sympathetic name he could trust and saw McDonald's, KFC, and Hilton. But no Motel 6. Being a cheapskate, Mike stayed at a youth hostel.

Funny thing, at the same time as all this took place, my ex gave up her consumer fetish. Suddenly, spirituality swept though our household faster than illegal immigrants vacating a meat packing plant when the Border Patrol appears at the main gate.

In just one day, she became enamored with bald men dressed in robes, meditation, and incense burning. She left our marriage and went overseas to the Far East. She returned with a reverence for nature, Tibetan chants, and a divorce attorney. Now she resides in a posh, grandiose, post-divorce island estate where she constructed a meditation garden with a gong that sounds every ten minutes.

Now, back to our story . . .

The next morning Mike woke up to begin the search for the customer who bought the case of Bud. Mike had a simple marketing plan: Solicit referrals from the happy new customer.

After an arduous journey via train, rickshaw, bicycle, yak, and finally elephant, Mike made his way to a tiny, deserted village. He went to the nearest hut, knocked on the door, and called out loudly, "Who ordered the case of Bud?"

A calm, serene, spiritual voice responded, "Come inside, Mike."

Mike, surprised someone in the village knew his name, hesitated. Then, with a bit of salesmen's courage, he opened the door and looked inside at a dark room. A single flickering candle sat on a low wooden table and cast soft shadows on the bare white walls.

"Please come in," the voice said.

Mike entered and let the door close.

A wisp of smoke formed and a baldheaded elderly man, dressed in orange robes, mysteriously appeared. He hovered in midair, sitting cross-legged, behind the low wooden table. He gestured for Mike to step forward and be seated.

Mike sat on a rug across the table from the hovering being and said, "How do you know my name?"

"My friend, I know all." The elderly man smiled. "I am the Magic Swami . . . you inquire about Raj Chang."

"Nice to meet you, Swami. . . . I don't know the dude's name, I just know he lives in this village."

"It is Raj Chang you seek. He is at the infirmary, a short walk along the road. Everyone is there because a large plane arrived carrying many good things from America and people from Hollywood. Come, we go together."

So Mike and the Magic Swami made their way to the infirmary where a huge mismatched collection of Hollywood stars, medical personnel, villagers of all ages, news crews, and government officials stood in the hot, broiling sun waiting for information regarding the health of village leader Raj Chang.

There was lots of angst and anxiety among the crowd, especially when the conversation and speculation turned to global warming. There was assorted shouting, yelling, pushing, and disorder. There had not been so much stress in the village since the British showed up 150 years earlier to grow tea and make people buy opium. Rumors ran wild about Raj Chang, his Avian Flu, and that it was all connected to global warming.

Nobody really knew the truth about anything because not enough data had been collected. Although some people claimed to have spoken to people, who claimed to have spoken to other people, who mentioned they heard about an American movie named "inconvenience," made by a former U.S. President.

However, nobody knew what inconvenience was because they

were too early in the consuming cycle and were still in the *need* portion of the hierarchy. However, the *want* portion was not too far removed, and it would not be long before advertising guys and credit counseling girls became members of their tiny village community.

Anyway, there was a rush to unsubstantiated opinion and wild exaggeration. Some people claimed, via "knowing," that "a twenty-foot wall of water would soon crash though their village like the monster waves at Pipeline."

Others, who also "knew," yelled back angrily, "No, Hawaiian television detective Magnum P.I. would never let the evil Pipeline monster ruin our village."

The only thing that could be agreed to was that everyone was exhaling carbon dioxide, sweating, and that Raj Chang was still inside the infirmary.

The scene reminded me of the eight people living inside Biosphere 2 twenty years ago. You remember—the ones who donned blue jump suits and were going to live two years in a sealed, self-contained, glass-enclosed, pseudo-Earthlike environment, completely cut off from all outside support. The futurist habitat was thoughtfully located somewhere in the deserts of Arizona under plenty of sunshine.

According to multiple Internet sources, some rich oil well heir put up $150 million to build the enclosed 3.5 acre building which included a rain forest, insects, mammals, an "ocean," fish, lagoon, farm land, and a wave-generating machine.

All of this money and effort were going to produce more "knowing." It is important to note that ants were not included as part of the original manifest of occupants inside Biosphere 2.

The situation inside airtight Biosphere 2 deteriorated rather quickly and soon the eight bio-prisoners found themselves stuck inside an oxygen-deprived, hothouse environment. It was similar to being seated on John Travolta's jet airplane wing at 15,000 feet, without the cool and refreshing breeze.

However, in the spirit of mission, the trapped biospherians persevered for the duration of their contract because it was deemed okay to pump oxygen into the building to keep the residents breathing.

The residents could have improved their standard-of-living, but they had not formed a bio-union and therefore they were unable to collectively bargain with the management forces located outside the walls of Biosphere 2.

So, they soldiered on with only ants as company and became hungrier each day. As a matter-of-fact, the biospherians became bio-skeletons because food production failed. I have reason to believe they were living on a diet consisting of algae, lichen, and the occasional "outside food source smuggled inside."

At the time the situation was characterized as, "friction among the human inhabitants."[7] Friction, in spite of the excitement of being dubbed "bionauts" and being composed of "a team of specialists right out of *Mission: Impossible*: a systems engineer, a physician, two biologists, agricultural scientists, [and] a computer systems expert."[8]

Two important things were learned inside Biosphere 2. First, the inhabitants could not stop exhaling carbon dioxide, and second, they spent a lot of time arguing and blaming each other for the overabundance of ants that had the run of the joint.

As proof, I offer this top-secret transcript I obtained:

Biospherian No. 1: What are you doing?

---

[7] What Is Sustainability, Anyway? Prugh, Thomas; Assadourian, Erik. World-Watch September/October 2003.

[8] What Is Sustainability, Anyway? Prugh, Thomas; Assadourian, Erik. World-Watch September/October 2003.

Biospherian No. 2: I'm picking the ants out my alga and lichen soup.

Biospherian No. 3: You know No. 2, it was 4 who let them damn ants inside.

No. 2: I told you not to call me No. 2.

No. 3: Well, No. 1 doesn't mind. And besides, it was 4 who let in the ants.

No. 4: I did not! It was 6!

No. 6: Shut up 4. It wasn't me. It was 3. They were inside his Earthshoes.

No. 7: Okay, who is releasing methane again!? I can smell it! We all have to get along, you know.

No. 8: Don't hyperventilate 7! You're sucking all the oxygen out of the room!

No. 7: Shut up 8 or I'll exhale more CO2!

No. 8: Listen 7, you're getting too big for your carbon footprint. If I still had the strength, I would squeeze your head like a tomato.

No. 5: Did someone say tomato? Gosh, I would give anything to taste a tomato—even canned or frozen.

No. 2: Damn ants! . . . I'M HAVING A MELTDOWN.

The secret Biosphere 2 transcript, and my divorce, confirmed my theory about a third human invention: Arguing—which is a tragic offshoot of buying and hitting—or living in a confined space with other people for longer than two days.

The failure of the environment in Biosphere 2 also suggests something else—perhaps a force bigger and more powerful than humans, perhaps even omniscient, maybe one that rises and sets each day, is at work regarding Biosphere 1, our Earth.

Oh, by the way, eventually a theory was floated that El Nino was responsible for the self-sustaining environmental failure of Biosphere 2. That, and Y2K.

And now, the rest of the story . . .

Someone, dressed like a doctor and who appeared to be an authority, came out of the building housing Raj Chang. He held up the case filled with Bud empties and yelled something in Chinese/Indian. There was jostling, yelling and pushing, and boos from the crowd.

Then someone led the crowd while they chanted, "Death to Bud!"

The man on the deck of the infirmary held the Bud package, filled with empties, high over his head. With a show of disgust and indignation, he threw it into the seething crowd where it was set upon and stomped by many men. In a moment of unbridled passion the entire crowd was caught in this frenzy and all were yelling, "Death to Bud!"

That is, except for three wise men who said, "What is Bud? We don't know what Bud is. We need to know more about Bud."

Mike got nervous. He leaned close to Magic Swami and said, "Dude, why are these people angry?"

"They 'know' America poisoned Raj Chang with the evil liquid in those cans."

"You mean Raj Chang drank that beer and is sick?"

"Yes, he drank all 24 in one sitting because he wanted to be like the cool Americans he saw on television commercials."

"Well, Swami, he over-consumed—he's been on a bender," Mike replied. "Tell them to give Raj Chang an aspirin and lots of water. He will be okay."

Magic Swami nodded that he understood. Then he floated above the crowd toward the doctor, who stood on the deck of the infirmary, and spoke to him. The doctor nodded and went inside the building. The crowd stopped yelling, continued to sweat and breathe, and waited.

About an hour later, Raj Chang emerged wearing only his lungi and bamboo hat. He stood on the deck smiling, waving, and shielding his eyes from the bright sun. The crowd went wild and then stepped away as Raj Chang made his way down the steps to be greeted by his family. His wife and 17 children rushed to gather around him.

Sighs of relief and joy raced through the crowd. Everyone hugged, kissed, and laughed. Even John Travolta, dressed in his red tutu and high heels, was at peace.

Raj Chang wanted to meet the American who knew how to save him from his hangover agony. He saw our hapless beer salesman and waved for Mike to join the celebration. Mike made his way through the crowd and shook Raj Chang's hand.

Then the most powerful event on Earth happened.

As Raj Chang introduced his family to Mike, the baby blue eyes of Sanya Li and Mike met in slow motion—love at first sight.

Someone in the crowd noticed Mike and Sanya Li smiling at each other and shouted. The crowd erupted with cheers, clapping, and high-fives. Everyone was even more delirious with excitement. Some even shouted wedding plans.

Mike wanted to impress his future father-in-law so he said, "Mr. Raj Chang, in my country we have learned to respect the environment and recycle. You can recycle those aluminum cans for money and it's good for the environment. It's all about sustainability."

Raj Chang nodded. He said something to his youngest son, Raj Chang Junior. The boy listened, his eyes lit, and he scampered about collecting the flattened Bud empties—seems his father mentioned a Playstation 4.

Raj Chang's wife pulled him close and cupped his ear. She whispered she bought condoms for him to use. You see, she discovered that adding more Chinese/Indian people to her family impinged on her husband's ability to earn spare rupees and yuan. Now she wanted buy things like a Jaguar, a face lift, and a Wonder Bra.

The Magic Swami serenely floated above the entire scene, seated in his cross-legged yoga position. He looked down and saw that it was good. He smiled, bowed his head, and opened his arms as if to embrace all below. Then he whispered:

"Love is the most powerful human emotion and triumphs over all human inventions, including buying, hitting, and arguing. Love will be the reason humankind grows and flourishes. In spite of your wayward ways, love for family will guide humanity toward a sustainable future. . . . All you need is love."

Epilogue

Yesterday, I received a communication from the chief of the lost Borneo headhunter tribe. He transmitted this final smoke signal and drum message:

You can now reach me via chief@borneoheadhunters.com. We are desirous to trade our shrunken heads for Budweiser, a Lexus for my wife, and for my daughter—Guess jeans, low-rise—just like the kind Anna Nicole wore.

Joe's Place

I turned my aging gray Buick Skylark into the dusty parking lot of a rundown concrete building that sat alone in the hot sun. It had a flat roof, beige paint that had peeled, and two small windows protected by metal security screens.

A hand-lettered sign, painted on a plywood panel, hung above the scuffed front door. It announced the name of the bar: *Joe's Place*.

My muse is named Joe. I figured to have a meet.

Joe is retired and runs the bar to pay his bills. A long time ago he was a professional wrestler who used the stage name Mr. Intellect.

Sadly, Joe had to give up a promising wrestling career after his first match against a shemale wrestler named Fabulous Moolah. It was a match billed by promoters as a battle royal between brains and beauty and it was a doozy.

Unfortunately for Mr. Intellect, his dreams of wrestling stardom were dashed after Fabulous Moolah vigorously performed a pile driver, reverse chinlock, and crippler crossface on her unworthy opponent. After he received his fourth body slam in the first round, Mr. Intellect was unable to get up off the mat.

While Mr. Intellect was passed out and spread-eagle, Fabulous paraded around and administered more indignities by shouting through a megaphone that a Vulcan Mind Meld proved Mr.

Intellect's head was empty.

The pain and humiliation caused Mr. Intellect to permanently hang up his purple tights and seek solace in a faraway place. Joe left the squared-circle stage and tried to join the French Foreign Legion. However, because Mr. Intellect's fighting reputation proceeded him, the Legion claimed they were closed to new volunteers.

So Joe chose the next best option and became a security guard at the Musée du Louvre in Paris. He spent the next 35 years standing guard five days a week in the room where da Vinci's *Mona Lisa* painting was exhibited.

Joe's sole duty was to watch people who looked at the *Mona Lisa*. He was not authorized to speak to the public and he could not leave his post during work hours. Part of Joe's new job was easy—he did not speak French and he did not drink coffee.

Unfortunately for Joe, he was fired after years of silent service because the museum installed security cameras and did away with the human element. Joe is still bitter.

I shielded my eyes and blinked as I entered the dark bar. The heavy door closed behind me, and I let my eyes grow accustomed to the dim light.

I walked to the counter and said, "Hey, Joe."

A bald, skinny, elderly man returned my fist bump. "Nice to see you again, Joseph. What'll ya have?"

"The cheapest bottle of beer you got."

He pulled a cold one from his refrigerator, popped the cap, and set it on the bar. I took a swig and looked around. The joint was empty.

"Joe, why do you keep this place so quiet?" I asked.

"What do you mean?"

"You don't have anything in here. No big screens. No jukebox. No sports or music. Not even a dart board."

"I'm too cheap to invest in entertainment infrastructure . . . and I looked at the backs of heads for 35 years. I want people to talk to me."

"I understand how you feel," I said. "Conversation is a good thing and I'm glad you're not like my ex."

He smiled and nodded.

"Joe," I said, "I need to explore my muse so I can better understand women. Are you in the mood?"

His demeanor changed and he studied me like a barkeep deciding to cut off a customer who had too much to drink.

"Listen Joseph, I spent a long time in Paris," he said. "I don't want to talk about women."

"But," I replied, "I don't want to talk about your time with Mona, I just want to know what makes you tick. Since we are good friends and can't get rid of each other, I insist we talk about it."

I took the last swallow of beer, set the empty on the bar, and studied Joe's craggy face.

"Besides," I said, "nobody else is going to have a conversation with you—I'm your only customer."

Joe tossed my empty into the trash and wiped the bar with an old smelly towel. As he put the towel underneath the bar, I thought to ask if it was the same towel his manager threw into the squared circle during his bout with Moolah.

Joe must have sensed that I wondered about the towel. Either that or he was a great mind reader.

"I know what your thinking," he said. "That's not the same towel. . . . Now, before we proceed, would you like a second beer?"

"Sure."

He put it on the bar and said, "Since you came all this way to see me, I'll talk—but don't bring up the body slams or I'll drop the conversation."

"So you'll lower the boom if I get out of line?" I asked as I stretched my neck.

"Yeah."

"Okay, I won't ask you about your ring time with Moolah, but I would like to ask one related question."

"Go ahead."

"What was going on between you two . . . was it that skinny guy, fat girl romance thing?"

Joe furrowed his brow, wagged his bony index finger at me, and said, "I never had sex with that woman. Now stop with Moolah or I'll go Robert Conrad and knock you off that stool."

"Okay, calm down," I said. "I'll change the subject. . . . What's the big deal with the *Mona Lisa* painting—why is it so important that you had to stand guard for 35 years?"

"It's the most valuable artwork in the world. A watchman was required because the museum did not want to pay the premium to insure it for an appraised value of $100 million."

"Dude, a $100 million?"

"That was the value in the '60s. Today it may be worth more than $750 million. . . . It's no ordinary piece of art."

"Well, gotta tell you Joe, the girl in the painting looks ordinary to me—maybe even homely. . . . And did you ever notice she is missing her eyebrows and eyelashes, not to mention that creepy smile?"

"You're missing the point, Joseph," he said. "It's Leonardo's magnum opus. The painting is an important symbol of the Renaissance."

"The most valuable magnum opus ever painted? . . . And just why is that?"

Joe looked at me with his smart guy Mr. Intellect expression. "Because it represents a great accomplishment in the world of art."

After a moment I said, "I remember the ring announcer said Moolah had achieved a great accomplishment after your manager threw in the towel."

Joe's smart guy look disappeared and he clenched his teeth.

"Sorry, buddy," I said. "I didn't mean that. . . . How about you give me another?"

Joe liked making sales more than clenching his teeth. He got a beer from the refrigerator and set it on the bar. Then he went to his cash register, rang up the sale of three beers, and placed the tab in front of me.

"In case this conversation wanders into no-man's land again," Joe said, "I've got your final bill ready."

I downed some and said, "Come to think of it, Mona Lisa looks kinda like Fabulous Moolah."

"If you persist, I'll cut you off and force you outside."

I fingered the tab and checked the total. Three bucks—and I had a ten spot in my billfold.

"Sorry," I said. "I don't know why I keep bringing that sore spot to your attention. . . . Say, did you ever figure out who the Mona Lisa is?"

"Nope, but there are several theories. Two interesting ones explain the painting as a self-portrait of Leonardo da Vinci or she represents a femme fatale."

"You mean de Vinci was a cross-dresser or it's a picture of a seductive woman who lures men into dangerous situations from which they cannot escape?"

"Exactly."

"Joe, I've got news for you . . . that means da Vinci was a cross-dressing femme fatale."

"I don't understand."

"Well," I said, "all art carries secret messages from the creator. That's why it's fascinating to study creative works because you can explore the dark recesses of the artistic mind and postulate theories as to why the creator is a madman."

"Or," he said, "you can make stuff up as if you are an amateur, bozo sleuth."

"Does that explain why mysteries like *The Da Vinci Code* are so popular?"

"I cannot say because I don't read fiction mysteries," he said. "But I read somewhere the author of that book made $100 million."

"Dude, a $100 million for writing a book with da Vinci in the title?" I stared at my beer bottle. "A $100 million insurance for a painting by da Vinci . . . I'm connecting the dots on your naked cranium."

I developed a strong urge to uncap my sharpie and draw lines on Joe's head, but I figured he would object. I took a swig of beer and contemplated the $100 million coincidence. Then I said, "Maybe I should change my name to J M da Vinci."

Joe ignored me. He continued to work, putting away clean glasses and slicing limes. We did not speak for some time.

He finally put away the cut limes and knife and said, "I did figure out what Mona Lisa's smile is about."

"What's that?"

"It was the same enigmatic look Moolah gave to me just before I got my first body slam."

"You sure you want to go there?" I said, secretly hoping Joe had forgotten his pledge to boot me from the bar. "I thought the smile was all about the feminine mystique."

"No—Mona Lisa's expression is the same expression a woman has when she has you by the short hairs."

"Ouch. . . . So you theorize the *Mona Lisa* model had da Vinci by the short hairs?"

Joe stopped wiping the bar top and looked me in the eye.

"Yes, because it explains why he did not paint eyebrows and eyelashes on her. It was his secret message to men—don't let women get hold of any short hairs."

"You got that right."

Joe was a good muse and knew when to keep quiet. I don't know how long it was before I came back.

I picked at the label on my bottle and just about had it pulled off without damage.

"What do you think about her . . . the Mona Lisa?" I asked as I pulled at the last bit of stuck label. It tore.

"After 35 years, I can't get her out of my mind."

"That's just like your final Moolah body slam—it lives forever on the Internet. . . . Come to think of it . . . the video of brains versus beauty might be more famous than the Mona Lisa painting—it certainly has had more views."

"I don't think that is possible," Joe said. "Nothing on YouTube will surpass the Mona Lisa . . . ever."

Joe's mouth twitched and he bit the inside of his lower lip. Then his eyes grew misty.

"Are you okay, Joe?"

He turned around, grabbed a paper towel, and wiped his eyes.

"Joe . . . did you love her?"

He nodded Yes.

"Is that why you went to see her everyday?"

He nodded Yes and I heard a stifled sniffle. I wanted to go behind the bar and put my hand on his shoulder but Joe had strongly warned me in the past that he was the only person permitted on his side of the bar.

"It's okay, bud," I said.

"She was a loyal woman," he said. "Stayed with me for all those 35 years." He turned and faced me. There were no tears and he seemed to have recovered. "Even though we didn't speak, we communicated. Her eyes told me everything and she was a great listener—never said anything unkind or condescending—unlike Moolah."

"Yeah, once Moolah got that megaphone in her hands she couldn't stop telling the world how beauty beat brains. It was embarrassing."

"I could have lived with the embarrassment," he said, "if that's where it ended with Moolah. But she inflicted so much pain on my body that I had to have spinal surgery—not too mention the sciatica I still enjoy."

"You enjoy sciatica?"

"Of course not," he said. "It was an ugly side effect of getting involved with a beauty like Moolah—it's my living scar from a bad relationship."

"I can top that, Joe."

"How?"

"Dating is sort of like the death penalty for men who wish to remain single," I said. "If you date, eventually a woman will get you roped into a relationship and you're no longer single."

Joe shook his head No.

"Bear with me," I said. "It's as if you're in the wrestling ring . . . grappling . . . leveraging . . . winning . . . and suddenly you're on the receiving end of a pile driver and being single only exists in some distant past life."

"That's why I stayed with Mona Lisa for so long. She never once hurt me."

"Yeah," I said, "even though Mona never said a word, she was a good woman compared to that spandex-wearing shemale who gave us a double martini of spinal trouble and sciatica—but I gotta tell ya Joe, sometimes I wonder if we made the right choice. . . . Perhaps we should have gotten involved with someone who was alive."

Joe wiped the bar top with his smelly towel and did not reply. He put away the towel and leaned on the bar.

"Joseph," he said, "we all keep the face of a loved one in our mind so we can think about that person and our love—even if we are far away, or locked inside a prison cell, or if the loved one has left our world for good."

"Yes, we do."

"And does it matter if she is ordinary or homely?"

"No, not at all."

"Then," Joe said, "that is why the Mona Lisa painting is a masterpiece. It represents the feelings of a man who loved her and it was painted so that man could remember her for all time. It is an iconic symbol of love . . . which is why we live."

"So we keep trying?"

"Of course," Joe said. He reached below the bar and pulled out the old smelly towel. Then he tossed it at me and said, "That's why God gave us a heart."

Does Poetry Matter?

Dear Sara,

Some time in the future, when you read this, people may tell you poetry does not matter.

But today, on your seventh birthday, you are like a love poem—beautiful, sweet and innocent. And faster than I want, my little girl is growing to be a young woman.

Much too soon, you will embark on a fantastic voyage to live your own life. A life rich with opportunity and potential. You may invent a better way to feed, clothe, or heal people. You might work to end inhumanity and unfairness in the world. Perhaps you will become a mother and rear wonderful children of your own.

The skeptics, naysayers, and pessimists, will shout the days of innocence and frilly fun will be nothing but a fond and distant memory. They claim yours is an uncertain future. These doomsday seers admonish the world is coming to a catastrophic end—a suffocating and horrible destiny due to war, intolerance, disease, God's wrath, famine, environmental destruction, or a myriad of other terrible causes.

I must write the truth to you, young Sara. The world can be a harsh, cruel, and unforgiving place. There are times when I believe the skeptics are correct—that poetry does not matter.

It is man's inhumanity to man which worries me the most. You inherit a world where suicide martyrs are honored when they kill innocent people—an act of racism and prejudice.

Humanity has battled these demons many times throughout recorded history. Your grandfather's generation fought against hateful violence—the killing of six million by the Nazis and the vicious atrocities committed by the Japanese. He, and many like him, got out of landing craft at places like Normandie and Iwo Jima, so our lives would be free of ugly hatred. When it was over, many hoped the world would never again see such horrid destruction.

But only a short time later, my generation faced war in Vietnam, and 50,000 American boys died. Good boys, who may have changed the world for the better or may have become my friends.

After this war, more than two million people were killed in South Asia by cruel dictators who came to power. Dictators whose legacy is a museum display of stacked skulls—skulls of fathers, mothers, children, and anyone deemed unworthy to live. It was another ugly time of ethnic and political cleansing.

Now, a new generation fights against those who promote another ideology of hatred and intolerance. Only history can say if this effort will be in vain, like Vietnam, or worthy of the accolades bestowed upon your grandfather's generation.

The repetition of vicious acts of inhumanity throughout history lends credibility to the skeptics' argument that poetry does not matter.

Optimists argue technology may save the day and that humanity will survive and prosper. However, pessimists counter that making the world smaller and smarter may accelerate our troubles.

It is important to remember that many people have done tremendous good, and sacrificed all, to make the world a better place. Against all odds, they fought the good fight against evil and injustice. Such people are with us today and will be born tomorrow.

My dear Sara, no matter what path you choose, you will face threats and danger. You must remain vigilant and prepared to protect those you love.

Keep your feet on the ground. Do not get lost in the clouds. Let integrity, humility, and compassion be your guideposts—they will remain faithful, when others do not.

Do not feel afraid of the future. Go with confidence in all you do.

For, you see Sara, I am certain you will meet a special boy. A good boy, with his heart on his sleeve and hope in his eyes.

One day this special boy will write a poem.

A poem only for you.

And then, my dear Sara, poetry will matter.

Your loving father.

The Magic One

There is nothing wrong with your brain. Do not adjust your eyes, your lighting, or your glasses. For the next ten minutes I control all thought that enters your mind. If I want to make you cry, I will. If I want to make you laugh, I will. Sit quietly and read because I control all that you think. You are about to experience awe and mystery from the inner mind of undergraduate Fisher.

Cue the black-and-white guy, dressed in a suit and smoking a cigarette. He puffs, smiles, and says:

"Man struggles daily to understand his place in the cosmos, to become a better person, a worthy citizen. This is the portrait of one such man, a child of the '70s and a fan of TV and movies, and his journey to understand his place on planet Earth. . . . Also meet the Magic Swami, his travel guide on this voyage of discovery."

I was totally stressed about writing my last college essay as an undergraduate at FGCU. After four years of university study and expense, I was gripped by the fear: *How will student J. M. Fisher end his collegiate career?*

It was the worse case of writer's block I'd ever encountered. Absolutely nothing came to mind as subject matter for the challenging assignment, *Portrait of Self as Citizen*. Every pen I seized was out of ink, every pencil tip broken, and my cats would not get off the computer because they were playing on-line games disguised as dog characters. The only idea I had for the assignment involved opening a beer and watching old television programs on Nick at Night. It was one of those frequent times when I wished I was as cool as a celluloid hero.

The fact is, I did not want to examine my life and my potential legacy. I figured just waking up and examining the unwanted wrinkles on my face were enough bummers to consider each day. And, I had little to show for my 50-odd-years—just a bunch of old calendars, beer bottle empties, loser horse race trifecta tickets, and a pile of dirty laundry.

However, because I'm a part-time egotist, I wanted my headstone to have a message besides, "I told you I was sick." If I didn't rewrite the rest of my life, who would pen my obituary—my ex?

And, just who would care to read that piece of fiction? Certainly not me.

But, I had absolutely no legacy ideas.

I needed a drink, a cigarette, and a meet with The Magic Swami—the guru of all that is wise. I had no doubt that he would know what to do. The Magic One and I go way back—in fact, a little over two years. I met him when I called about a Yellow Pages advertisement which read: *Free Advice and Life Coaching.* The Swami and I immediately became friends, even though I, as a cheapo, only took advantage of his freebies.

I called Swami, got voice mail, and asked for an appointment at his earliest convenience. Shortly thereafter, I received a text.

It read: *Magic Swami busy. Meet Sunday at 3:30 a.m. FGCU Reed Hall 207+, door marked Higher Education.*

The Swami was an early riser, so I stayed up all night and hung out at a local watering hole making bets on the Greyhound races via closed-circuit television. At 3:00 a.m. I'd gambled away my winnings and was out of dough, so I headed to my appointment with the Magic Man.

I arrived and entered a brightly lit and quiet Reed Hall. Nobody was around, not even the night shift cleaning crew. I went to the second floor and found Rooms 207 and 208, but I couldn't find 207+, or any door marked Higher Education, even though I was at a university.

I knocked on the door to Room 207. There was no answer. I knocked on the door to Room 208. No response. I circled the floor twice and still did not find my objective.

I retrieved my cell and dialed Swami, figuring I might hear his phone ring. The call did not go through and my phone displayed the message, *Unknown Call.* I verified the number and re-dialed. Same result.

Then I surmised that he made a text typo, so I tried all of the doors—every one of them on the second floor, and then, on the first floor. All doors, except to the restrooms, were locked. I walked back to 207 and knocked again. No answer.

By now, I was five minutes late, and I worried that Swami might cancel my appointment. I was also tired, so I sat against the wall and considered my options.

Things didn't look good—I couldn't find Room 207+, or a door marked Higher Education. There was no one around to ask for help. And, the phone number did not work. It seemed my meet was cancelled, and as a result, so was my final essay, which I now titled *Portrait of a Doomed Undergraduate.*

As I contemplated my unlucky predicament, I looked up—and that's when I saw it—a door—in the ceiling. A small hand-lettered sign on the door read: *207+ Higher Education.* It was in the middle of the hallway and right above the doors for Rooms 207 and 208. I'd walked the corridors of Reed Hall many times, but I'd never seen the door in the ceiling. Then it dawned upon me—I'd never seen a door in a ceiling, anywhere.

The problem was how to reach the door? It was 10 feet above the floor and it had an electronic keypad. I knew from my Reed Hall walkabout there was nothing obvious that I could stand on to gain access. Then I remembered a door, in the first floor Men's Room, marked *Custodial*. I went downstairs and tried it. It opened.

I entered and looked around the closet-sized room. There, on a set of gray metal shelves sat several rolls of toilet paper, a soap dispenser, plastic trash bags, bottles of cleaning supplies, and a gallon of industrial-strength ammonia. I also spied, partially hidden behind two unopened cartons of toilet paper, a quarter-full fifth of Jack Daniels—and even better—a half-full bottle of Gordon's Dry gin.

Yeah baby.

Best of all, in the corner, against the back wall, behind several push brooms and buckets with mops, stood a six-foot step ladder.

Perfect.

I grabbed the Jack Daniel's, the Gordon's, and the ladder, and carried them to the ceiling door. I took a swig of whiskey and climbed to the second-from-the-top step of the ladder, reached up, and turned the doorknob. It was locked, but the electronic keypad lit with a red glow.

I thought about a number combination and pressed 1234 and Enter. Still locked. I tried several more combinations that came to mind, all with the same result. Then I tried the numbers of my birthday, my telephone, my address, and the last four digits of my social security number. Nothing worked. I tried 411, 911, 666, 42, 36-24-36, and even my secret pin number. Still locked.

I climbed down, sat against the wall, and wondered what to do. The problem of a meet with Swami had all the hallmarks of life—that is, occasional happiness interrupted by long periods of struggle. Just finding that door was a big accomplishment and then the ladder. But now, I was stumped by a lock combination.

I needed to loosen up and zen-out to find a solution to the problem. Raising awareness, or spreading my complaints around like manure, would serve no purpose. And anyway, who would listen to my cries for help—the creatures of the night?

I had to get outside the box so I lit a cigarette.

Thank goodness the university anti-smoking Nazi's are asleep.

I smoked half my cigarette and thought about numbers. There were so many possible combinations. I went up-and-down the ladder several times and tried various alternatives. I searched my brain, thinking of numbers that were important—account numbers, ages, sports scores, carbon footprint numbers, flight numbers, ID numbers, credit card numbers, and anything I could associate with the concept. A lot of ideas came to mind, but none added up to an open door. I really needed an accountant or a mathematician to show up.

I took a sip of Jack Daniel's. The whiskey tasted good as it rolled down my throat. I looked at the bottle and read "Old No. 7 Brand." Um, a new number to consider. Maybe the secret was to use only one number—which would be a far simpler solution than pi.

However, my enthusiasm was short-lived. I pressed the seven key and nothing happened. So I pressed 007. No lucky number for me.

I sat down again and remembered an old scrap of paper that I'd carried in my billfold for more than twenty years. The clipping was of sentimental value and contained quotes of inspiration. I pulled it out and unfolded it.

I read the first quote, *"There is nothing more difficult to take in hand, more perilous to conduct, or more uncertain in its success than to take the lead in the introduction of a new order of things—Niccolò Machiavelli."*

On this scrap of paper was something I had written long ago:

Patent No. 5153830.

I scurried up the ladder and typed the numbers on the keypad. The red glow turned green and I heard the lock unlatch. I pushed on the door and it easily opened upward.

Bingo dude.

Beyond the door was a black void. I steadied myself on the doorjamb, climbed to the top step of the ladder, and cautiously stuck my head through the opening. The black void slowly came into focus as a dark nighttime sky lit by a million tiny stars. As my eyes became accustomed to the darkness, I noticed a large Oriental carpet hovered in midair, nearby. A wooden table stood atop the carpet. Two candles, in brass candle holders, sat on top of the table and glowed with a mystic aura.

A calm and reassuring voice said, "Welcome, Grasshopper. Please have a seat."

I looked around and saw no one. I grabbed a hold of either side of the doorjamb and pulled myself up and through the doorway. As my body moved through the opening I became weightless. I floated over to the carpet and assumed a cross-legged yoga position on one side of the table.

The candles flickered briefly and a thin wisp of smoke appeared. The smoke materialized into the form of a human being and a moment later he was across from me—the Magic Swami.

He wore a simple purple robe tied together with a purple sash. He was a small, thin man, bald and clean-shaven. He looked absolutely pure and selfless, and also ageless, as he sat in a cross-legged yoga position.

He smiled, as if contemplating the silence of the forest, clasped his hands together, and bowed his head slightly. I felt a most serene, harmonic and spiritual feeling—even though cheesy New Age music was not playing.

"Good morning," he said.

"Magic Swami, great to see you, but I don't know if I should say good morning, or good night." I rubbed the two-day-old growth of whiskers on my face.

"You are my first appointment today. Lots of FGCU students need my assistance before graduation."

"This is some office you got, Magic One. . . . But, I gotta tell ya, there were a lot of hurdles to get up here."

"We only meet with those who are truly motivated."

"I almost gave up, but I used my powers of word association. I always had one more idea to try."

"Yes, the magical power of word association. Quite simple really—some might say patently simple."

"Speaking of magical powers Swami . . . can we use yours to see who wins tomorrow's daily double?"

"Ah, my power of magic," he said. "We can talk about tomorrow, but no gambling tips, my son."

I looked around and took in the view. We were just above Reed Hall and I could see parts of the university campus. Our carpet rose slowly into the still, cool night air. Oddly, I felt no fear of heights or my situation.

"Magic One, it seems like we are rising into the sky? I need essay ideas, not a mystical flight of fancy."

"Grasshopper, we've embarked on a journey to understand your time on Earth. Reflection will help you with your assignment."

I thought about my life. There were so many memories and I wondered where to start. I looked at him and decided I needed to change the subject.

"Swami, sometimes I wonder if I should go on—I've had a good run."

"Often times people avoid self-reflection, my son."

"So this is a journey of self-reflection?"

"Yes and no. This is a time of reflection, like a solitary walk on the beach. It's also a moment for you to imagine the future."

"Wise One, I'd like to imagine the winner of next week's game between the Pistons and the Lakers—you know, just in time to call my Vegas bookie."

"No, Grasshopper. We can only discuss your potential legacy."

So, it really was time for me to consider my life and not gambling odds. Swami hovered serenely. My mind raced with jumbled memories which collided with thoughts about my future. We floated on the carpet, slowly rising like an old elevator. I looked down at the campus which spread out below.

After a long time, Swami said, "My son, graduate wisdom will soon be yours."

"But Magic One, I've first got to write my final paper about my purpose on Earth. The only theme idea I've had is to be a film hero, like Charlton Heston in *Ben-Hur*—a tough, masculine, warrior dude."

"I'm not sure you are the *Ben-Hur* type."

"Okay, maybe I'm not Academy Award material. . . . How about as Heston in *The Omega Man* . . . the movie where he was the last guy on Earth and played chess against a bust of Caesar while crazed nocturnal, light-sensitive, albino mutants chased him?"

"No—the only zombies in your life are old memories chasing you."

"Okay. . . . How about this idea . . . humankind is regressing—we can't manage our place in the cosmos . . . what if I'm the last educated human on Earth, like Heston in *Planet of the Apes*?"

"Nope."

"But I need an exit strategy for my life and a great ending line for my paper—something like Heston's, 'Take your stinking paws off me, you damned dirty ape.'"

Swami arched his right eyebrow and crinkled his forehead. I surmised he was surprised by my nearly-graduate wisdom—or my extensive knowledge of Hollywood trivia.

"Your final exit strategy is always necessary . . . but presiding over the demise of humankind is not a good ending for your paper."

Neither of us spoke for a minute or two.

"I've got it!" I said. "How about like Heston in *Soylent Green?* That was the last movie made by Edward G. Robinson before he died. Coincidently, his movie character chose euthanasia to go home and was made into a green wafer to feed the starving masses. In the *Soylent Green* future there was no food because of global warming and overpopulation. It's just like what humanity faces today."

"You seem to be preoccupied with being the last human alive, my son. Do you see yourself as the savior of humanity?"

"That's probably my part-time ego—the part that wants a hero's legacy and the need to rise to a better ideal."

Swami and I floated higher, as if lifted by a hot air balloon. The city lights of Fort Myers spread out down below. I was warm, comfortable, and not afraid.

"Swami, I'm trying to figure out the continuity of my life, and where it leads. . . . Why was I put here . . . if I'm not to be a hero, what am I—just a simpleton in the mass of humanity?"

"No man is a simpleton, and not every man gets the recognition he deserves. As far as continuity, you must also look at the opposite . . . the discontinuity . . . those surprise life obstacles that cause a change in direction."

"Boy, that is me—I'm always running into obstacles. Sometimes I feel like *The Fugitive.*"

"What kind of obstacles?"

"The usual suspects . . . time, money, energy . . . bill collectors, ex-wives, bum family members . . . seems like life is a marathon of broken field running."

"Yes, but that is a strength. You always keep going, Grasshopper."

"So that's the continuity in my life—a pair of Nike's?"

Magic Swami presented his serene smile and remained silent.

"What about my inner demons, Swami—and I don't mean my man boobs."

"You mean your fascination with beautiful women, booze, and gambling?"

Boy, the Swami hit me hard—there was no fooling him. I fidgeted and cracked my neck. I wanted a cigarette but the last one was gone.

"Magic One, are you going to replay my life mistakes?"

"Could you have done things better, my son?"

Swami now had me in a logic headlock. I needed to change the subject to escape his uncomfortable wrestling hold, so I tried to think of a positive attribute I possessed.

None came to mind.

Finally, a long, lost thought surfaced, and I said, "I've always considered integrity to be important."

"Yes, somehow you avoided the urge to self-destruct—just like humankind. What values do you admire in others?"

"I guess the most important one is personal responsibility. To do what is right when no one watches. Fiduciary duty and all that . . . endurance . . . to carry on when circumstance demands surrender, or I want to quit."

"Integrity and endurance are good ideals. They are the bedrock of clear thinking and good decisions."

"Swami, they also offset my impulsive, self-destructive desire to pursue ill-conceived goals and manipulate people in nefarious ways."

"That is good, my son."

We sat quietly as our carpet climbed higher. I looked far away at the lights of Florida down below. I don't know how long I stared away. Magic Swami was a patient and good swami.

Finally I said, "I have experienced many troubles in life because people don't behave with integrity. Why don't people have integrity?"

"Human beings have freedom of choice—they choose their behavior. Bad choices create bad situations. That's why endurance is important, so you don't quit in the face of trouble, conflict, and hardship."

I nodded my understanding.

He said, "But endurance is not to be confused with stubbornness. You must adapt to avoid failure."

"I know stubbornness, Swami. On my last losing streak, a voice in my head continually called out bad bets. It wouldn't shut up until I lost all my money. I really thought I had a permanent case of bad karma."

"My son . . . what about the other little voice inside your head, the one that calls out when you see someone who needs help?"

"I gotta tell you Swam, the voices in my head are really busy. Someone is always talking . . . sometimes I just don't have the energy to listen."

"Yes, there is lots to do."

"I wish the little voice would be quiet."

"You must remember that voice is you—"

"I don't get it Swami. The little voice is me?"

"Yes. Every time you called for help, someone answered. Now your voice echoes back through others. Remember all the people who have helped you."

I sat quietly while the memories slowly came to mind—my family, teachers, friends, strangers. Even my cats helped when I felt sad. I remembered people, with very little, who stopped to help me. The memories brought tears to my eyes. I thought about the times I never said thank you. Even Magic Swami appeared to be unhappy.

After a long time I said, "Swam, someone always encouraged me with a good word, a pat on the back, or lifted me up and brushed away the tears. There have been many good people in my life."

He nodded his understanding and I felt better. We sat in silence.

After a long pause he asked, "What does your small voice say when you see people in need, Grasshopper?"

"Stop and help . . . But, I have finite resources . . . and I can't commit to more than I can do."

"You can always find a way to help, my son—just like those who helped you."

I looked into space over Swami's left shoulder and considered his wisdom. A new worry came to mind.

"What about all those ants I burned with a magnifying glass when I was a kid?"

"You can make up for past transgressions."

I pulled out my empty pack of cigarettes and said, "Can I bum a smoke?"

He declined with a polite shake of his head. "Smoking is bad for you, makes you prematurely age. Do you want to leave before your time?"

"Sometimes I think yes, I've had enough of the misery on Earth. There is so little I can change and there are so many worthwhile causes. I don't know where to start."

We were higher in the sky now, and moving faster, like an airplane. The dark, curved line of Earth's horizon and the city lights of Florida were way down below.

"Do you want to be an activist for ants, my son?"

"I feel as if many activists are like television evangelists, Magic One."

"Yes, you must use discretion—only some causes are worthwhile."

"I don't want to be a cynic Swami, but it seems many are just after dough. They claim the cause will fail unless I write a check.

Especially those running for political office and other professional cheaters."

"They prey on your emotions."

"You got that right, Swam. . . . I'd like to give them a global warming burn from my magnifying glass. It would be fun to watch the crooks try to escape my hot lens of sunshine." I pressed my fingertips together and added, "Come to think of it, I'd go after despots, evil dictators, and their minions—Hitler, Pol Pot, Stalin, Edi Amin—the entire group of humanity who torture, kill, and imprison. Let's add Mao and his Cultural Revolution to that rancid pile of humanity."

He chuckled and said, "You sound like an activist, ready to change the world."

"Yeah, and I could do it right from here with just a hand-held magnifying glass. Like Archimedes said, 'Give me the place to stand, and I shall move Earth.' I say, give me a magnifying glass and I'll show you productive activism—courtesy of my burning ray of justice."

"Son, that is admirable. But, you can't go backward to correct the wrongs of humanity—that is a different adventure. You must go forward and work for change in today's world—without your ray of burning justice."

"I'm bumming, Swami. There is so much I could do with that little magnifying glass."

Swami and I communed peacefully with darkness around us. We picked up speed, like a rocket headed for orbit, and crossed into space. The sun lit the South American continent below us.

The moon loomed closer and in a moment we sailed past. The Earth set on the horizon. It was a tiny blue orb set against the blackness of the void. I saw the Earth was a small and fragile place hovering alone. I felt sadness about all the hardship humanity had endured.

"Swami, when I look at little Earth, I feel compassion and humility for the good people who struggle to make a place for themselves and their families, and for those who struggle to make it a better place. . . . Even the ones with whom I disagree. If my imagination ruled, there would be no more fights, lies, and greed."

"That's why the Earth needs good people—to work for the good. But, you must be practical . . . you can't wear rose-colored glasses."

"What about the bad things that happen, Magic One? I once stood in the incineration room at a concentration camp. The ugliness and horror were awful."

"Earth is a place where many good and bad things can happen. How did your experience change you?"

"Oh my—it charged my emotions about totalitarianism and fascism—it was firsthand experience of man's inhumanity to man."

"I know those feelings too, my son. Humanity has much to discover and the universe to explore. But, there are those who will commit atrocities, promote injustice, and behave with greed."

"Swami, why is humanity like that?"

"The human race is a rhizome—it extends different beliefs, ideas, and philosophies in all directions. Some of them are good and need to thrive. Some are bad and need to die on the vine—that is why you must work for the good."

I looked down at Earth, with her moon hovering just a short distance away, both bright spots in the sky below us, round and smooth. I saw a perfect world, without the bumps and imperfections of humanity. All of the good and bad were now just a blue and white globe, with a dark half and bright half.

It was the bright half, the side in the sun, that was most beautiful and worth the fight. A place which creates men and women who carry the fight to the dark side—to insure the protection of the good. 'Ol Swam really had me thinking.

"Wow, Swami, it's amazing. I had absolutely no idea I could see so far and so clearly."

"You are progressing well, my son."

"Magic Swami, did you ever take this trip with other people?"

"Yes. Galileo, Copernicus, Verne, Einstein, Asimov, Clarke, Sagan and many others have journeyed to this viewpoint."

I admired the scene for a while. He hovered and waited for me.

Finally I said, "Swaminess, I know there are no easy answers. I've learned most decisions are a compromise, based on incomplete information, competing agendas, and emotion. But it's important to get up each day and sally forth."

"Graduate wisdom will soon be yours, Grasshopper."

We zoomed onward. I saw the entire solar system, held together by a small, ordinary sun, shepherding Earth and her sister planets through the blackness and emptiness of space. Then, I spied something out-of-place.

I pointed and said, "Swami, what's that over there? It looks like a piece of metal."

He turned and said, "That is the *Voyager One* spacecraft, launched in 1977. It's the farthest manmade object from Earth, now 9.8 billion miles from your sun, my son. . . . *Voyager* is an ambassador of humanity. It carries a gold record which contains a library of sounds and images of life on Earth."

"Swami, I believe that is a most significant accomplishment—think about what it took to send a library, documenting life on Earth, on an infinite journey into deep space—there is a little bit of each one of us riding on that spacecraft."

He clasped his hands together and said, "Librarians are very important, my son. They organize all knowledge so you can remember the past and not be condemned to repeat it."

"What about my personal library of bum memories that chase after me like zombies?"

"You must forgive . . . like us Swamis."

"Yeah, but I can't. It's a personality flaw—like smoking and drinking—I just can't seem to forgive those who have trespassed against me."

"I know it is difficult. Even I, the Magic Swami, must work to forgive." He gestured with a sweep of his arm, "Remember all of this will pass—and one day—you will look back with fond memory at what had been your life."

"Can I get a do-over, Magic One?"

"We don't give do-overs. That is why lessons learned are important."

Swami gave me a long easy stare while I turned his words over in my mind. Like a great teacher, he knew when to speak and when to wait for his student. My conversation seemed to be coming to an end, but I still didn't know how that final sentence would read.

I opened the bottle of Gordon's and said, "After recalling my bum memories, I'd like to get off this nonsmoking flight and stop in at a joint for a drink."

I offered him a shooter.

He waved his palm and said, "Grasshopper, will you feel proud that you made the world a better place? Or, will you let yourself be tormented by bitterness and anger?"

I sat and thought for a very long time. As I replayed my life, I felt like I was inside a dark movie theater, and I felt very alone. I figured maybe this was the end so I took the last swig from the bottle of gin.

"Swami, reflection about one's life purpose is a lonely journey."

He sat peacefully and quietly. The candles flickered briefly. Swami turned to his right and nodded his head once.

Then, for the first time since meeting him, I heard an outside sound—soft music from a faraway piano. Gradually, the music grew louder. A black man, dressed in a tuxedo, materialized. He sat at a grand piano and gently caressed the black-and-white keys.

And then slowly, a beautiful lady, wearing a white dress, appeared and smiled at me. She looked familiar, but I did not know who she was. The entire setting was bizarre—the piano player, the gorgeous brunette, the Magic Swami, and me.

I looked at him and asked, "Who is she, Swami?"

"She is every woman you ever loved, my son."

I looked at her again. She changed just a little and I recognized her as my first girlfriend from the 3rd grade. She smiled and changed into a girl I dated during my first year of college. Then she changed into the woman who later became my ex-wife. And then, I recognized her as Mrs. Peel—my English flame who went out with me one night in Paris.

I turned to Swami and said, "Of all the gin joints . . . in all the places . . . in all the worlds . . . she walks into mine."

Magic Swami did not respond. I turned to look at Mrs. Peel.

She smiled at me and said, "Darling, I know you will become the scribbler you always desired. . . . You must go back and write about what you have learned."

Swami gently said, "You've still got time, my son."

Mrs. Peel turned to the piano player and put her hand on his right shoulder. He looked up at her.

She said, "Play it, Sam. . . . Play . . . *As Time Goes By.*"

The piano man nodded and softly played the song. The candles flickered, and very slowly, one by one, they all disappeared—the piano player, the beautiful lady, and the Magic Swami—as the music faded away.

Cue the black-and-white guy, dressed in a suit and smoking a cigarette.

He puffs, smiles, and says,

"Portrait of Self as Citizen—a man—and a life. That eternal struggle between the dark and the light, between the good and the

bad. And proof that Man's greatest attribute is the desire to do what ordinary men do—rise to fight the good fight another day.

The Magic One . . . submitted for your approval . . . from the Twilight Zone."

hello, little a

hello little a on the page
isolated and naked
no one to support you when you look to your left

you stand solo, my little friend a

holding so much potential
with nothing yet to say

waiting for the spark, the lightbulb, the noun to be
a sprout, a serve, a sunrise
it's all on your shoulders
my little friend a

what about the tiny e?
this is a letter worthy of a name
declared the poet, cummings, e. e.
yes tiny e, you have your place
as fifty percent of me

oh, to be o, to be full and complete
you have your place in the cosmos
circle, ring, oval, loop
no hole, no empty, no void, no zero

wonder what it's like to be u?
an american idol, a diva
or denizen of twitter
a bauble and babel of our pop culture

we are all much like you, little a
no one wants to be alone
to be alive just as one

we all seek embrace
because little a
we all need a place

and what would you be
my little friend a

if you were I?

Hook, Line, and Sinker

Like Finn and buddy Sawyer

    biking to our favorite beach spot
    steel grip on prized fishing poles
    we chatter along the long roadway

Anticipating

    line finally wet
    lunker swallowing the bait
    the shout: "Fish on!"

Nothing else matters

    young, no license required
    we sneak past
    the No Fishing signs in life

Summers melt away

    lunker stories turn to whoppers
    and fish net stockings
    beckon as catch of the day

We tell each other

    "Yes, we'll go real soon now"
    as fisherman are prone to lie
    while reminiscing with beer

Old Polaroids show two lads

    skinny as fishing poles
    holding fish like men
    and a bucket filled with more

I study the faces—

    lost and gone long ago
    I smell the stink, the bait, and the sea
    as if it were today

Somewhere

    life became a knot
    a backlash
    an entanglement to undo

An ebb tide runs now

    that barracuda called time
    hungry
    relentless

I wander lonely

    to the sandy shore
    gaze at the distant
    blue horizon

Feel cold

    and think about
    the old man
    and the sea

And remember

    my favorite fishing pole
    my friend Sawyer
    and my ex-wife

Parted

    like the big ones that got away

A lady walks alone along the beach

    wrapped in a yellow vest, white blouse
    blue jeans, auburn hair
    barefoot, like a young boy going fishing

She startles my solitude

    New Year's Eve smile
    soft, sweet voice
    "Do you like fishing?"

A wave rolls to shore

    "Yes, I did, long time ago"
    I look to the sea and back at her
    Her lips say, "I always wanted to learn"

Sunrise

    in the misty light
    alluring eyes sparkle
    gold earrings dangle and flash

I take the bait and say

    "Let's have a beer
    and I'll tell you
    a fish story or two"

Them 'Skeeters

Inspired by the Mason Williams poem, <u>Them Ants.</u>

How 'bout them 'skeeters?
Ain't they a bunch?
Flyin' round my head
Lookin' for lunch

Them ornery 'skeeters
Carryin' a disease
Buzzin' in my ear
Ain't them a tease?

Them greedy 'skeeters
Down by the crick
Waitin' around
To give me a prick

Them meanie 'skeeters
Makin' me itch
I sure need to scratch
No wonder I twitch

I don't like them 'skeeters
Not one bit at all
Cuz as a nudie
They eat me raw

But, I'm gittin' even
With them evil 'skeeters
Slappin' and squishin'
Them blood-suckin' cheeters

Lookie them 'skeeters
Ain't they mad?
Wrapped my buck-nekked body
With plastic from Glad

About the Author

J.M. Fisher and Renee reside on Sanibel Island, Florida,
in a house owned by Mr. Cheeti—a cat.

For the latest, please visit

jmfisher.com

Made in the USA
Lexington, KY
13 March 2015